WILLY

# WILLY

## *A Novella*

## By I. J. Singer

## Translated by
## Joshua A. Fogel and Linda/Leye Lipsky

Hamilton Books

Lanham • Boulder • New York • Toronto • London

Published by Hamilton Books
An imprint of The Rowman & Littlefield Publishing Group, Inc.
4501 Forbes Boulevard, Suite 200, Lanham, Maryland 20706
Hamilton Books Acquisitions Department (301) 459-3366

6 Tinworth Street, London SE11 5AL, United Kingdom



British Library Cataloguing in Publication Information Available

Library of Congress Control Number: 2020901421

ISBN 978-0-7618-7182-8 (pbk.)
ISBN 978-0-7618-7183-5 (electronic)

# TABLE OF CONTENTS

# INTRODUCTION

## Linda/Leye Lipsky

The novella *Vili* (Willy)[1] written by Yisroel-Yeshua Zinger (Israel Joshua Singer) has been overlooked by reader and critic alike. Except for Sholom Groesberg's doctoral dissertation on Singer's novellas,[2] it has garnered neither close reading nor scholarly exegesis. This translation seeks to put to rights this state of affairs, and, by making *Vili* available to the English reader, to broaden its potential for interpretive interest and reflection. While it has neither the multi-generational sweep nor the moral *gravitas* of Singer's family sagas, it is refreshing in its lack of pretense. The narrative arc is a skeletal one, and a familiar one at that: a rebellious son leaves his ancestral home to find adventure among strangers and lose tradition and family along the way. This stenographically-figured human drama is enacted on a foreshortened proscenium. It is a novella, but in no way is it a small novel: its themes are timeless, its struggles archetypal. A father and son duke it out, and, in the process, lay claim to the reader's imagination. We hope this introduction affords the reader a port of entry to this neglected treasure.

Anita Norich's critical biography of Singer's oeuvre, *The Homeless Imagination in the Fiction of Israel Joshua Singer*[3] has been roundly hailed as a work of incisive critical acumen and as a comprehensive and unstinting chronicle of the facts of Singer's life, down to each editorial and critical entry in the *Forverts* (Forward) and *Literarishe bleter* (Literary pages). She has noted every geographical move from childhood on, from Biłgoraj, Lublin province, to Leoncin to Radzymin to Warsaw, to Kiev, to Moscow, back to Warsaw, to New York, and to many havens in between: "Wandering is a countertext to Singer's own itinerancy."[4] Indeed in *Vili* exile works at the levels of both thematology and authorial posture. Norich offers a compelling case for his central metaphor: "Singer sees no possible geographical or psychic locus for the Jewish imagination. . . . Wandering and dislocation, as both Jewish and modern tropes, emerge as central themes of Singer's writing."[5] This applies with equal force to *Vili* wherein the Modernist theme of exile—geographical, existential, and intellectual—and the shifting contours of landscape and topography inform the narrative. Expatriation, both self-imposed and enforced, drives the tale. Homelessness, loss of community, and transience are the eponymous protagonist's fate. His father Hirsh, on the other hand, experiences deracination from his homeland, with his roots irremovably entrenched in the Divine Intelligence.

Irving Howe, in his essay, "The Other Singer," went a long way in educating a presumed readership to Singer's skillful artistry: "I. J. Singer built his work upon spacious architectural principles. . . . He mastered, as few Yiddish writers have, the problems of construction special to the 'family novel.'"[6] The same obtains for *Vili*, writ small. Groesberg maps Singer's twelve novellas along a temporal continuum, situating *Vili* in the middle sub-group, where he posits that certain features have been "improved": "With time Singer became more proficient in techniques of plot . . . and . . . smoother articulation between narrative portions."[7] *Vili* evinces a mastery of tools specific to novella-length fiction, such as appropriate and delimited character development and compressed and elliptical diegesis. No room here for attenuation or discursiveness. Singer's belletristic design is buttressed by his widely-admired architectonic workmanship.

T. S. Eliot famously named Ezra Pound *il miglior fabbro*, the better craftsman, in an epigraph to *The Waste Land*.[8] So, too—*mutatis mutandis*—does Bashevis defer to the superior artistry of his older, celebrated brother on many occasions: in dedications, in interviews, and, ultimately, in his Nobel Prize address: "I dedicate these pages to the memory of my late brother, I. J. Singer. . . . To me he was not only the older brother, but a spiritual father and master as well. Although a modern man, he had all the great qualities of our pious ancestors"[9]; "When I got the Nobel Prize, I felt my brother standing there with me on the stage in Stockholm, sharing the prize and celebrating the victory of Yiddish."[10] In the speech itself he notes a comprehensive education: "As a child I had heard from my older brother and master . . . all the arguments that the rationalists from Spinoza to Max Nordau brought out against religion."[11] More tangibly, Singer taught his brother to put together a sound story, a tale well told: "I consider him a great master of construction."[12]

Yet, neither history nor memoir records an extended fraternal appreciation of the Singers' sister, Hinde Esther Kreitman, except to note, without true recognition of her talent, that she lit "the first literary spark"[13] in their family, her words, it seems, mere tinder to the hard, gemlike flame of her brothers' creativity. On the Genesis recurrent model of up-ending and reversing primogeniture privilege, I. J. Singer was the one to achieve fame and adulation before Kreitman did. In her autobiographical novel *Deborah* (*Der sheydim-tants* [The devils' dance]), she presents a trenchant portrait of Singer in the character of Mikhl. He is judgmental, scornful, mocking of her aspiration to study: "When Michael [Mikhl] . . . found his sister crying, a psalter in her hand, he laughed . . . boisterously. . . . [H]e snatched this opportunity of poking fun at her, calling her a fool for staying indoors, for poring over the Psalms."[14] Despite his respect for his brother, Bashevis never addressed him, waiting for Singer to make the first overture,[15] as he feared his brother's opprobrium. Singer's accomplishment cast a pall over Bashevis's early career, while Singer himself seems to have survived the anxiety of Kreitman's influence.

The storied photograph of the group of writers (see below) known as "Di khalyastre" (The gang), from left to right: Mendl Elkin, Perets Hirshbeyn, Uri-Tsvi Grinberg, Perets Markish, Meylekh Ravitsh, and Singer himself. They are seated, posed variously, looking off in different directions, leaning warmly into each other, Markish reclining comfortably, their territorial imperatives happily violated in a spirit of camaraderie. There sits Singer—ramrod erect, arms crossed, his steely gaze impossible to evade, a rigid affront to the group's loose confederacy. The "reader" of this photograph might infer from the body language that Singer is, at worst, aloof, taciturn, restrained by a cold intellectual reserve. But armed with Kreitman's and Bashevis's "composite" character sketch above—the insecurities of the siblings doubtless an influential factor—one might deem Singer supercilious, scornful, mocking, imperious, and dismissive. (That he received fellow writers warmly in his literary salons in both Warsaw and Brooklyn might militate against this

Figure 0.1.    Members of the literary and artistic group Di khalyastre, founded in Warsaw in 1922 (from the left): Mendl Elkin, Perets Hirshbeyn, Uri-Tsvi Grinberg, Perets Markish, Meylekh Ravitsh, and Singer himself. This photograph was taken by noted photographer, writer, and friend to this group, Alter Kacyzne, at his country retreat, in Swider, a resort town outside of Warsaw, which had an "air of a bohemian enclave." Marek Web, ed. *Poyln: Jewish Life in the Old Country: Alter Kacyzne.* New York: Metropolitan Books, Henry Holt and Co. In conjunction with the YIVO Institute, 1999. "Introduction," p. xiv.

portrait). If passion be measured by the length and volume of one's hair—the photograph famously shows Markish to be the most hirsute of these long-haired poets—then this image suggests Singer's lack of ardor. A lukewarm Laodicean in various literary spheres and political pursuits, Singer, along with this novella *Vili*, eludes an easy taxonomy. And accordingly, we will reveal Singer to be variously Modernist and anti-Modernist and *Vili* to be in a class of its own.

Hence, *Vili* is best understood in terms of what it is not; it does not handily fit classical categories. Mendele Moykher Sforim turns his realistically and ruthlessly drawn types to satirical and censorious advantage. In this tradition, Singer's painful childhood experience with the rabbi of Radzymin has inspired the villainous Rabbi Meylekh of Nyesheve in *Yoshe kalb* [16] as it has breathed life into his portrayal here of

Reb Hirsh who certainly typifies the most brutal traits of a small-minded Hasid. However, unlike the sustained anti-Hasidic broadside in *Yoshe kalb*, the satire in *Vili* flickers on and off, to be spent certainly in the last scene of reconciliation and reward for the father, if not for the son. Hirsh's human folly—a literalist's enforcement of the letter of the law, fired by an overweening vanity—is presented in the story in ever more parodic terms. In the end, he finds—through peripety—undeserved recompense, that is, a deferential and admiring congregation of fellow believers. This flies in the face of the post-Heraclitan paradigm of character-as-destiny which has animated so much of Western literature. What is more, how can the unnamed towns in *Vili* compete with the satirical force of a "Kabtsansk"? Far from Perets's "rehabilitation" of Hasidism,[17] *Vili* is mere flaccid social commentary, defanged of any biting censure or prescriptive recommendation: there is no retribution exacted for the many instances of men behaving badly to women.

Is *Vili* a picaresque tale? Its itinerant hero, one of the "young ruffians" (p. 33) is not, by any fair assessment, a rogue, or a *picaro*. Volf takes his episodic travels—the army's far-flung barracks, the rural outback, the American city and village—to his personally-achieved frontier, but his inscrutable, morose nature ensures that there will be no tilting at windmills here. *Vili* is certainly not a classic *Bildungsroman*, as its normal avenues of learning are resisted: Volf's *kheyder* (religious school or classroom) is the meadow, the farm, and the stable, an idyllic revision of the scene of instruction. In any case, there are two Jamesian "centers of consciousness," or foci: as the narrative pivots, readerly attention shifts from Volf to his father, Reb Hirsh, and back again. Volf is the rare eponymous *agon* who must share center stage with his antagonist, that is, his more voluble *paterfamilias*. Once in America, both Volf and his father redouble their respective efforts to rebel and to push back. His enlisting in the Russian army is less an instance of pride of country than it is a measure of his need to escape the clutches of his monolithically pietistic father and to spurn his spiritual patrimony.

While there are various social strata and working classes represented, *Vili* is not a proletarian novel, subsumed as it is in the non-partisan effort to define what is lost and what is gained in immigrant passage to the new world. While Singer was drawn to socialism for its broadly collectivist and humanist mandate, he was but a fellow traveler. Yet his wife Genia defends Singer's radical and deeply informed views about

Soviet Communism, the class struggle typified by the plight of the textile workers in Lodz[18] against the widespread impression that he was a turncoat: "Nissan *was* my husband. . . . He had poured all the enthusiasm of his revolutionary faith into that character."[19] Singer subscribed to the writer's union, the *Literatnfareyn* or Writer's Club, in Warsaw, where he "fervently justified the regime"[20] until 1918 when he moved to Kiev, with Genia and became deeply disappointed in Bolshevist universalism; he moved to Moscow in 1920, and returned to Warsaw in 1921. His first novel, *Steel and Iron* is unrelievedly political and anti-Stalinist, based on his own experience in the Russian army and in the interregnum between Russia's internal revolutions.[21] This book was decisively panned: this example of an ideologically "failed alchemy" was deemed politically formulaic.[22] Hence, resisting both type and genre— satire, *Bildungsroman*, picaresque, political novel—as noted above, *Vili* is nonetheless a tale worth telling.

Any writer of the early decades of the twentieth century must confront his or her positionality within or against the canon of Modernism. Accordingly, the reader must situate *Vili* in the context of Singer's accommodation to, or rejection of, the Modernist agenda. Ruth Wisse notes that Singer's may be the "briefest flirtation with literary modernism on record . . . but as the least enthusiastic member of the circle ["Di khalyastre," see below], he was the first to repudiate its ostentatious radicalism."[23] While flirtation is an active, if coy, coquetry, Singer evinces a passive, if weak, capitulation to the seductions of the wide-ranging movements of Yiddish Modernism. Singer's was a selective implementation of high Modernism's hallmark creeds of impersonality and self-sufficiency, not their wholesale purchase. While in *Vili* Singer engages many Modernist themes—existential exile, the limits of knowledge, urban estrangement, spiritual desiccation—his aesthetic is decisively pre-Modernist, as he eschews non-naturalistic stylizations for realistic chronicle, symbolist suggestion for mimetic verisimilitude, and imaginative speculation for positivist certainties. As a studied rationalist, he was temperamentally at odds with the declamatory excesses and expressionistic indulgences of his radical collectivity, "Di khalyastre" (The gang), so named by Hillel Tseitlin.[24]

Both Singer's literary affiliations and, more frequently, his non-adherences determined the aesthetic choices that shaped *Vili*. Singer found himself in Kiev to help defend Yiddish secular culture and all its local inflections against the threat of erasure by Russification. The *Kul-tur lige* (Culture league), along with its organ *Zamlung* (Collection), was a hub for Yiddish educational, political, and literary activities—including the unrealized "Universal Jewish Museum" and the "little" magazines such as *Eygns* (One's own) and *Oyfgang* (Arise)—until its mandate was subsumed under the bureaucratic machinery of the *Yevsektsye* (Jewish section) of the Communist Commissariat. Singer was caught up here in the Jewish nationalist versus the global universalist, the specificist (*yidishlekh*) versus the generalist (*algemeyn-veltish*)[25] debate which raged across the pages of the above-mentioned journals and newspapers. He inevitably threw in his lot with the Yiddishists who saw the language as a robust conduit for class consciousness. Tenaciously guarding his ideological independence, programmatic about his rejection of programs, Singer demurred at membership.

To the Kiev "triumvirate"—Uri-Tsvi Grinberg, Perets Markish, and Meylekh Ravitsh—Singer was the fourth and odd man out,[26] even though he drew on the group's political sensibilities. If Singer borrowed the spirit of insurgency from the group, he would soon more than return the favor by lending them a wide readership, culled from the established enthusiasts of his work in the Yiddish press. Abraham Cahan, editor of the *Forverts*, had read the well-received short stories, *Perl* (Pearls), with which Singer leapt upon the literary scene, published in the journal, *Ringen* (Links).[27] Cahan subsequently enlisted Singer to be the Polish correspondent, "our man in Warsaw," and later to write a travelogue of post-revolution Moscow.[28]

Singer would go on to co-edit *Literarishe bleter* (Literary pages) in Warsaw from 1923. While Singer co-edited, with Markish, the inaugural issue of the almanac *Khalyastre*,[29] his Modernist proclivities were not hardy enough to endure until the second issue in 1924, published in Paris. The group "Di khalyastre" was a motley assemblage of literati and artists of wide-ranging location (Lodz, Kiev, Moscow, Warsaw, Berlin), political stripe (Bolshevism, Bundism, Yiddish Territorialism, Revisionist Zionism), and literary practice.

To the avant-garde stylings and idiosyncratic extravagances of his cohort, Singer mounted his own rearguard offence: his novels, short stories, and novellas are traditionally-fashioned and respectful of the Aristotelian unities of time and space; *Vili* proceeds in like manner. In his co-edition of *Khalyastre* his own linear short story, "In the Dark" or

"In Darkness,"[30] told in sober prose, stands out in high and conspicuous relief to the varied expressionistic wailings, lyrical flourishes, and hyperbolic dilations on the bloodied, harrowing and barbarous human condition in the volume. The title page ferociously proclaims its name in jagged, tooth-like typography.

The frontispiece presents Broderzon's poem about his *khalyastre* of adventurous, trail-blazing young folk, who overcome their horror and despair to wrest meaning and starward aspiration from adversity, *"Per aspera ad astra!"* Above this is Itsik Broyner's barely figurative rendering of a male *corps de ballet* in Modern dance-like flat-footed, squatting, angular postures. As writers were published in many concurrent magazines, a collaborative and magnanimous spirit prevailed: there is a prominent advertisement for *Albatros* (Albatross) under the "Table of Contents" at the back of the almanac. Markish's manifesto writ small on the first page of the almanac proclaims the program for the "confederation of anarchists" inspired by loss and anomie whose "measure is not beauty but horror," to which Singer could not consistently subscribe. This credo is short on literary regime—if we consider the almost contemporaneous *In zikh* (Introspectivist) Manifesto of 1919, where a meticulously-enunciated, impressionist aesthetic and praxis are drawn up—but long on burning determination and tempestuous riposte. A closer look at Singer's selections for the almanac is instructive: while he does not write this way, he acknowledges the legitimacy and necessity of these works in the Yiddish Modernist canon.

Among the works included in the almanac, most of which offer a blinding proliferation of exclamation marks are: Meylekh Ravitsh's Whitmanesque celebration of the human body in all its sensuous variations; Iosef Tshaikov's essay "Sculpture," in which he expounds the Jewish character of Constructivist, Futurist, and Primitivist sculpture; Uri-Tsvi Grinberg's thoughts on a Godless and loveless universe; Yoysef Opatoshu's *cri de coeur* on mob rule and the lynching of "Negroes"; Arn Glants-Leyeles's poem about a golden fish as holy grail which turns back on itself in spiral word play; and Perets Markish's jeremiad on the squalor of the poor. Into this mix of bold expression and forward-looking criticism, Singer offers his own *agitprop* tale, as noted above—written in Kiev in 1919—about Hirshl, a harried and lonely photographer beset by a demanding, slave-driving boss. Surprisingly, the narrative gives way to a technical exposition of the process of developing photographs, replete with chemical formulae, solutions, and equipment. It is Singer's most exquisitely Modernist moment: a self-reflexive and metapoetical exegesis of the artistic process itself. There are ekphrastic descriptions of studio photographs and charcoal sketches; Hirshl is an aspiring graphic artist himself, as was Singer.[31] His descriptive, bucolic settings in *Vili* evince a painterly sensibility: he describes the meadow with "errant bits of snow" (p. 25); the wildflowers and blades of grass are depicted in colorized detail. The Symbolist correspondences of "In the Dark" have no equal in *Vili*: the darkroom is a separate realm over which Hirshl resides as sovereign, the red light a discrete planet, the photographic negatives hide creatures that wait in ambush. The ambient luminosity of *Vili*, the scenes set *en plein air* daylight are a stark contrast to this unremitting darkroom tonalism.

Then there is *Vili* with its diachronic unfolding of events and its retrograde and commonsensical musings. Singer is constitutionally averse to a panoply of Modernist literary behaviors: the aestheticist decadence of *Di yunge* (The young ones), the purposeful defamiliarizations of the Russian Formalists, the deliberate temporal obfuscations of the stream of consciousness novelists, the playful inventions, coinages, and the phenomenological perspectivism—the "inner panorama"—of *Di inzikhistn* (The introspectivists). That said, *Vili* does reflect the linguistic turn that philosophy and literature assumed in the post-Wittgenstein era: the boundaries of one's world are defined by the boundaries of one's language. To that end *Vili* exploits the limitations of both the spoken and the written word. Singer adroitly chooses silence as the most fitting of Modernist devices to highlight the unrepresentability of the human condition. Singer's family sagas—*The Brothers Ashkenazi*, *The Family Carnovsky*,[32] and others—are densely populated by a multi-generational cast of thousands. In *Vili* Singer presents a nuclear, intergenerational family unit with scant reference to Volf's more historic forebears. Volf's own brother, who consequentially brought the Torah from Europe to Hirsh's small prayer space in America, is not named, nor are his many siblings, nor are the villages where the scenes are played out. The *dramatis personae* comprise a very short list. Ancillary characters such as Volf's mother and wife are richly compact figures, occupying minimal textual space. This is not a well-upholstered novella: spartan furnishings, an austere simplicity which neither protracted description, distracting dialogue from peripheral characters, nor intrusive secondary or tertiary plot lines can serve to undermine. While Singer notes his childhood ability to hoard events of no significance,[33] *Vili* is denuded of superfluous or tautological details. The full attention of the reader is trained on the respective spiritual and spatial journeys, dislocations, and relocations of Volf primarily and his father secondarily, told in elliptical conversation. Speech is often labored. The silences loom menacingly: "[Volf] began to use . . . words which became familiar through the slow, muffled speech of the farmer and the drawn out sounds of the daughter. There weren't a lot of them—the words—that these folks used, a scant several hundred. Beyond that they were silent. Volf learned this speech as well as the quietude. . . . Just like the farmer, he tossed out words, askew, from one side of his mouth" (p. 57). The abridged sexual encounter transpires wordlessly, with tacit surrender.

By contrast, there is the Babel of tongues, in *Vili*, the various languages spoken—Polish, Russian, German, English, Italian and their respective dialects—both in Poland and America, the thick, macaronic texture of sounds. All this against the lowing of the cattle, the whinnying of the horses on the farm or the din, the clatter and the "ruckus" (p. 77) of the elevated train and the subway in New York city. After a moment of urban anomie, Volf regains his sense of self in a stock Modernist trope, the lonely crowd: "Carried along with the crowd, Willy crawled around somewhere, disentangled himself from the rabble, and in the midst of it all, sensing a greater intimacy to something from which he had been separated since childhood" (p. 78). Loosed of his native moorings, his sense of place, he awakens to his heretofore suppressed nostalgia: the food in a Manhattan restaurant is redolent of "Jewishness and the old country" (p. 77). The meal inspires an epiphanic moment, tempered with a modicum of poetry: "the chicken soup . . . small reflective pools of fat." Only then does he recognize that he has brought his past with him: it has traversed oceans and currents of social and historical circumstance. As Singer records the immigrant passage to the new world, any vestige of the Modernist project must necessarily be subverted by an historically and ethically responsible one, an inevitability, as Irving Howe sees it: "Yiddish modernism, precisely because it is Yiddish and therefore tied to a particular destiny, can never be as free and unburdened and gratuitous (or as irresponsible) as the modernism of Europe and America."[34] Amid the endless wrangles about the autotelic and formalist, versus the mimetic and social, functions of literature which presented themselves in the early decades of last century, Singer favored the latter.

Yet in the true precisionist spirit of early Modernism, that is, the "sufficient" image, character portrayal is essentialist and not evolving. Volf is as untamable as the wildest of his horses. Except for a short-lived appeasement and fleeting sea change in his letter to Volf, Reb Hirsh is as intolerant as the strictest of *melamdim* (teachers). Drawn in short-hand, in the spirit of caricature, what emerges is a morality play duel of predictable, dependable, and contending types: an advocate for a free and wanton communing with nature (Volf) meets his entrenched and obstinate opposition (Hirsh). Neither of these main players brook any negotiation with each other nor arbitration by secondary characters. While Singer's family sagas have their full range of emotions, the *dramatis personae* of *Vili*, with feeble and largely off-stage support by Volf's mother and wife, do not constitute a full complement of characters—barely enough on which to hang a narrative. Yet, this spare human drama is compelling by virtue of its crafted simplicity.

Singer was born into a rabbinical dynasty in 1893 in Biłgoraj, Poland. His father served for a time in Leoncin, near Warsaw, then in Radzymin, but had difficulty keeping a rabbinical post, because it required state certification and fluency in Polish. Until his late teen years, Singer had a rigorous religious education, but by seventeen he was already reading "contraband" fiction in modern Hebrew. His was an observant and scholarly household, a mixed marriage of Hasidim (Romantic-Mystic) on his father's side and Mitnagdim (Adversary-Rationalist) on his mother's, herself a daughter of the revered rabbi Reb Yankev Mordkhe of Biłgoraj. These star-crossed pedigrees caused Singer to bemoan in his memoir the "tragedy . . . that fate transposed genders in Heaven."[35] Not mincing words, Ruth Wisse notes the "Manichaean nature of the [Singer family] struggle."[36] In most of Singer's novels battle lines are fiercely drawn along this mystical/ intellectual divide, along with their respective attitudes and strivings. In *Vili*, on the other hand, we have all the messy truth in between. A binary typology of character in this novella soon proves unworkable. Hirsh is a Hasid, but he is no *tsadik* (righteous sage). He speaks of the Bible and business affairs in the same breath. He enjoins Volf's *melamed* (teacher) to "[b]eat him, break his bones" (p. 31). He goes from one remonstrance of Volf to the other. Volf is not his father's intellectual equal, nor is he armed with cogent barbs against him. Volf does not answer in kind Hirsh's Talmudic musings. No dialectical warp and woof of debate. No study-house conversations with their lilting expostulation and reply. Hirsh holds court about Halakhic observance and the Biblical passages on which they are based, but they fall on deaf ears. These dialogues are, properly, monological tirades. The formula above would dictate that the contending protagonist be a *maskil* (follower of the Jewish Enlightenment movement). Instead we have a "stand-in," an apostate, who props up his disbelief by citing the Bible. This "heretic" is introduced late in the narrative in the person of the American pharmacist, the "Litvak miscreant" (p. 100), with whom Hirsh enjoys sparring about Maimonides and the Talmud, admiring his sharp intellect: "Berating each other, rebuking one another for their respective unthinkable and untenable belief systems, the two men became very close."

In his study of the "cultural nexus" of Yiddish literature and Talmudic discourse, Jordan Finkin notes this inclination to "intellectually manipulate rabbinic texts."[37] The character of Hirsh, armed as he is with Biblical allusions and their Midrashic inventions, affords Singer the opportunity to showcase this convergence. Singer, the "boy philosopher"[38] had a prodigious and prolific career outside of *belles lettres* as polemicist, largely evident in his editorial pieces. Yet there are no "essayistic" interpolations to the narrative here. The ideational infrastructure must be arrived at through the novella's *mise en scène*, what is said or what is imagined, not by "importing" philosophies as we have with the nihilism of Turgenev's comparably intergenerational *Fathers and Sons*. Bashevis elucidates: "My brother always used to say to me that a writer should not mix the essay with fiction. . . . Dostoevsky . . . [i]n *The Brothers Karamazov* . . . suddenly inserts a whole essay on what a saint is and what a saint should be. . . . My brother always used to call this literary mannerism."[39]

Volf's lapsed Judaism is his father's dystopian nightmare: a collection of Halakhic transgressions and worse, his renunciation of study. Instead, he is a devotee of nature, its flora and especially its fauna. The very first chapter sets the tone for Volf's semi-apostasy: the rote recitation from the *Song of Songs*, the aping of his hapless *melamed* while ignoring his entreaties. The Biblical images are tangled into an inextricable knot, tripping him up. The trope noted in Singer's memoirs is even more stunning for its exploitation of Volf's object of sustained affection, the horse. As fledgling scholar, the young Singer sees himself as a beast of burden to the demands of Bible study: "At the age of three I am wrapped in a prayer shawl and harnessed to the yoke of the Torah."[40] Singer's fate as a recusant, a freethinker, an *apikoyres* (heretic) was sealed very early on: "cracks of doubt had widened into chasms of skepticism."[41] Volf, by contrast, "was not an unbeliever, and he knew that there was a great God in heaven" (p. 79). The double negative underscores the tenuousness of this conviction. Instead, Volf's love for his horses was steadfast and unbridled: he held onto their manes without the mediation of man-made straps of leather (p. 30). Singer, too, loved horses. His use of "In Harness" as a chapter title in *Steel and Iron* underscores the fate of the prole as work horse.

Volf's unnamed mother hurls the insult, "Is a horse to be your teacher? . . . You're going to grow up to be a peasant!" (p. 24). Volf wears this as a badge of honor. That Hirsh, writing a letter to Willy years later, allows his wife to write "at the edge of the paper" (p. 73), is indicative of her marginal status within the family circle. Her words make up for their paucity with the heartbreaking tenderness they betray. Women in the novella, including Wolf's sister, are not drawn with a sense of detail or distinction. The exception is the grotesque and colorful folk image of Willy's mother force-feeding a turkey on her lap, fattening it for the kill (p. 24). More maternal scenes of hen to chick, mare to foal ensue. Willy attends a birth, mimicking his mother's making her meat kosher before cooking, "as he rubbed the salt" on its "faltering . . . legs" (p. 28). These vignettes are richly *folkshtimlekh*, as Perets had it, "in a folk mode." Another folk-derived portrayal is the toothless stable and farmhand, old Roch, who was wont to whittle a pipe out of a tree branch, as he imparted his bits of homegrown wisdom. Another secondary character is Volf's wife, Esther. For Volf the attraction was sealed most viscerally: Esther smelled of "horses, the road, dust" (p. 52). The consensual seduction scene takes place offstage, controverting both Singer's own father who called both Singer brothers "pornographers" who "sell papers"[42] and the chairman of the *Yevsektsye*, Itsik Fefer, who, in a fit of *apparatchik* invective, tagged him a "rabbinical pornographer."[43] Esther's sensuality does not define her. She is loyal, compliant, submissive, willing to learn about the Biblical forefathers and ritual observance. Volf's mother and Esther, a motherless child, enjoy a warm and reciprocal relationship, the likes of which no blood relatives—save Esther and her father—enjoy. In his chapter on *The Family Carnovsky* in his book *Gemishte khasenes in der yidisher literatur* (Mixed marriages in Yiddish literature), Moyshe Menakhovski notes the particularly loving relationship between the two women from the moment the matriarch understood that her daughter-in-law Teresa followed all the laws of *kashrut* in the kitchen and, what is more, comported herself *yidishlekh* (Jewishly) in all spheres of her matrimonial life.[44] She removed her string of pearls and bestowed it on Teresa, as testimony to her unalloyed acceptance of the mixed marriage. Georg's father Dovid, not so much. Initially, this same family dynamic is at play *chez* the Rubin (later, Robin) clan. But Hirsh would soon come to "praise her [Esther] for her piety and called her 'daughter.'" This in turn would blossom into mutual admiration. Whatever limited strides they might have made toward defining their respective independent personhoods, Volf's wife and mother retreat into their default settings of domesticity, harking back to the literary portrayal of women of the *klasiker* (classical writers) according to Mikhail Krutikov "[who] were instrumental in ushering in the new moral and social order by means of their 'Jewish' virtues but they possessed almost no personalities and were reduced to their traditional roles after this task had been completed."[45] In *Vili* Singer offers an instantiation of Anita Norich's insight that "individual fate is . . . overdetermined by social and political restraints."[46]

The opening pages fix Hirsh as an irascible, sententious, door-slamming, abusive tyrant who sees no contradiction in citing the Bible even as he hurls invective at Volf: the moniker *balegole* brings with it associations of Hirsh's public mortification and low station beyond its denotative meaning, "horse's groom" or "wagon driver." Having inherited his father-in-law's country inn, Hirsh—"a city man, an assiduous student"—longed for the company of Jews in the village (p. 28). He wanted to be "a Jew among Jews" (p. 36), a refrain he uses both at home and in America. In America he will love the company of his *landslayt* (local compatriots), when he could not abide them back home. Volf is not a model of filial devotion: he is no Aeneas who carries Anchises on his back. Instead we have a son whose abandonment of his Jewish affiliation is tantamount to abandoning his father. Absent for years without correspondence, Volf ultimately does the right thing and arranges for his parents' emigration. Once in America, Hirsh suffers a series of indignities to his ritual observance, one more egregious than the next:

sleeping without a *mezuze* (an encasement containing parchment with the text of the *Sh'ma* prayer) affixed to the doorpost and eating meat without a *hekhsher* (ritual seal of approval), among others. He marks Willy's desecration of the Sabbath, with a rendition of the liturgy of blithe welcome to the Sabbath, the *Lekha dodi* (Come, my beloved), sung in the dirge-like liturgical chant of *Tisha B'av*, a solemn, commemorative holiday marking the destruction of both ancient Temples. In short order, Hirsh will come to respect the clean-shaven rabbi and find a *minyan* (quorum of ten men) with whom he can pray.

The reader might wonder how Reb Hirsh could be content with this pale facsimile of its European prototype. In his memoir, Singer railed against the "provincialism" of the "remote reaches of Leoncin" to where his father "transmigrated from Biłgoraj."[47] Hirsh's paradise in small town America is his Platonic form of the *shtetl*, or at least it is the site of its happy and successful embodiment. It is everything that I. M. Vaysenberg's *A shtetl* (A [Jewish] town)[48] is not. David Roskies terms it "an all-out attack on notions of communality, on the hegemony of learning and respectability that was said to characterize traditional Jewish society, on the supposedly inexorable bond that tied Jews to other Jews, analogous to the covenant that tied them to God." Roskies goes on to say that it "documented the centrifugal forces" that undermined the cohesive structure of the shtetl.[49] Antipodally, Hirsh's centripetal, inward-looking, solipsistic forces create a space of Jewish sodality, a throwback to Sholem Asch's personal squint on the *shtetl*,[50] where all— whether by parody or by wishful thinking—was well with the world. Hirsh brought his sententious, Bible-thumping ways with him to steerage, when, by all accounts and popular consensus, they should have been left far behind. This is America after all, where a transplanted *shtetl* is a grotesque and cognitively-dissonant construct.

Volf is conversant with the local vegetation, from spring flowering to autumn harvest, the foliage, the woods, the streams, the grains, the cycles and rhythms of the seasons, the texture and relative acidity of the earth which happily offers up its yield. Norich notes the attractions of the earth: "As if to contain . . . perpetual restlessness, Singer peoples . . . stories with characters who have a strong relationship to the soil. . . . They [here, she includes Volf] are . . . lovers of nature, physically strong, happy when engaged in agricultural labor."[51] His arcadian aspiration to commune with nature and, along with this, the deep knowledge of the local landmarks and indigenous crops, may have been inspired by the Jewish Society for "Knowledge of the Land," the *Landkentenish* movement of the 1920s and 1930s which promoted the salubrious and informed encounter with one's pastoral environment.[52] It inspired a Jewish nationalism and folkism through a sense of expansive rural space. "It is a fact," begins the inaugural issue of *Land un lebn* (Land and life) in December 1927, "that we Jews, especially from Warsaw, and also from the other larger cities in Poland are also far removed from nature. There will be many among us who . . . cannot distinguish between the simplest species of trees; who have no idea what stalks of corn or wheat look like; . . . who possess no sentiment whatsoever for nature and her wondrous creations."[53] Volf's entire life, his very marrow, is a redress of this situation; what is more, he brings it with him from the old country to America. The descent of city folk onto Willy's farm is reminiscent of these country jaunts and *Landkentenish* "tourism." The idyllic setting is a diversion from city and shtetl life and, for Singer himself, a reprieve from the oppression of study: "I'd glance through the *Book of Morals* and follow its fanatic rantings about the vanity of vanities that consumed the world and I would grow deeply resentful. . . . Every tree, grazing horse, every foal, haystack . . . called out to me."[54]

Yet the reconciliation of the last chapters of the book was ushered in by Hirsh's most tender, grateful, and loving letter—the sea change noted above—tearfully received by Volf. Hirsh cites here the Hebrew of Biblical image and homily, but when he needed to convey his emotional life, he "switch[ed] over to Yiddish": "To my dear son, the longing of my soul, the apple of my eye, the glory of your name in its beauty . . . like our father Jacob, when they brought him the news that his son Joseph was alive" (p. 74). He was uncannily able to communicate his love in a letter, when he could not do so face-to-face. This epistle may very well be the emotional centerpiece of the novella, one that precipitated Hirsh's reversal of fortune.

For all their small rapprochements, the chasm between father and son is too cavernous to span. Their respective universes—study and husbandry—run parallel, intersectionality an impossibility. The rules of *kashrut* are non-negotiable as is the "[b]itter discord . . . [which] ensued between father and son just like in years gone by" (p. 95). This impasse is fundamental, owing, in part, to a stylistic difference: "Willy was stingy with his words. . . . To every burst torrent of his father's speech he had a single word" (p. 96). Hirsh "regarded himself a man of substance, a master in his own home" (p. 97). Volf, by contrast, according to the father, "knew nothing of any real meaning at all" (p. 97). The good will created by his loving letter was soon to be but a distant memory. All spiraled downward into recrimination, embarrassment, and, inevitably, tears. Being deemed a scholar by people in similar circumstances gratified Hirsh no end. He strutted around, truly the "big shot" that he professed to be. His small personal house of prayer was Hirsh's newly-found personal territory, his *dalet ames* (literally, four hand-breadths, across whose boundaries one cannot steal). It encroaches on, and colonizes, Volf's own real and imagined space. While Volf's universe can exist alongside, and in happy interaction with, a gentile one, Hirsh's *shtetl* exists apart from the outside world, isolated. Volf is a lost soul at novella's end. Hirsh, by contrast, has found his true calling: to bring that old-time religion to his cohort of displaced and uprooted immigrants.

*Vili* is an eminently filmable story. Imagine, if you will, the histrionic Maurice Schwartz[55] as Hirsh, the novice David Opatoshu[56] as Volf and a Hollywood happy ending, complete with *dei ex machina*—Hirsh's congregants—to save the day. But wait. Instead, the film, projected in the dark theater of the Jewish soul, fades out to the novella's last scene. Camera pans to Volf: lost, rudderless, casting about in a turbulent sea of possibilities, restless, wanting to flee: "He thought hard about taking off from there, as he had years before from the town back in Europe, when he unexpectedly left one night from home and stole across the border" (p. 111)—as did Singer himself in his time of youthful rebellion: "I waited for my parents to close their eyes, then fled like a thief from the prison of the Torah, the awe of God."[57] Singer goes on to compare his father's exclusive life's work—a comprehensive "defense of Rashi"—to his own state of mind, which further bears a remarkable likeness to Volf's: "I was restive, on edge."

Fittingly, the horses have the last word: "The horses stretched out their necks to Volf, the better to be caressed by him, as they neighed in his direction, longingly" (p. 111). The ensuing cavalcade of events marches on ineluctably.

## NOTES

1.  In the collection *Friling* (Spring) (Warsaw: Farlag Kh. Bzoza, 1937), pp. 3–108, serialized in the *Forverts* (April 7–25, 1936); abridged version for *mitlshul* (middle school), ed. Zalman Yefroykin (New York: Arbeter Ring Mitlshul, 1948). Our translation follows the unabridged, full edition. *Vili* is the Yiddish title of the novella, the Yiddish rendering of his Americanized name, Willy. In Yiddish he is Volf or its diminutive, Velvl. Volf Rubin is dubbed Willy Robin by the sheriff who officiates at his wedding, at the end of chapter 5. In the opening pages of chapter 6, Volf calls himself Willy. For consistency and clarity, I will be referring to the eponymous hero exclusively as Volf in this introduction.

2.  Sholom Groesberg, *Israel Joshua Singer's Novellas: An Analysis of their Creative Elements.* Doctoral Dissertation, The Jewish Theological Seminary of America, 1991.

3.  Anita Norich, *The Homeless Imagination in the Fiction of Israel Joshua Singer* (Bloomington, Indiana: Indiana University Press, 1991). This is the only book-length study of Singer's oeuvre.

4.  Norich, *The Homeless Imagination*, p. 24.

5.  Norich, *The Homeless Imagination*, p. x.

6.  *Commentary* 31:3 (March 1966) pp. 76–82.

7.  Groesberg, *Israel Joshua Singer's Novellas*, pp. 78–79.

8.  (New York: Horace Liveright, 1922). This tag of the dedication is itself derived from Dante's words of esteem for Arnaut Daniel in Canto 26 of the *Purgatorio, The Divine Comedy*, thus extending the chain of allusiveness. Chief among Pound's recommendations was the use of the footnote to handle the hyper-allusiveness of Eliot's text, a practice rare in poetry, but implemented in Pound's own *Cantos* whose range of reference is multi-lingual and encyclopedic. Singer's abridged book, mentioned above, uses footnotes, *lehavdl elef havdoles* (literally: to make the distinction of a thousand distinctions, to acknowledge that the present context is very different) as a pedagogical tool. Many Polish and Slavic words are given their Yiddish translations, along with the translations of certain ritual observances which would have been outside of the purview of many American middle school children attending secular Yiddish schools.

9.  *The Family Moskat: A Novel*, trans. A. H. Gross (New York: Farrar, Straus and Giroux, 1950), unnumbered dedication page (*Di familye mushkat*, 2 vols. [New York: Morris S. Sklarsky, 1950]).

10.  Cited in Israel Zamir, *Journey to My Father, Isaac Bashevis Singer*, trans. Barbara Harshav (New York: Arcade Publishing, 1994), p. 57.

11.  Cited in Zamir, *Journey to My Father*, p. 163.

12.  Joel Blocker and Richard Elman, "An Interview with Isaac Bashevis Singer," in *Isaac Bashevis Singer: Conversations*, ed. Grace Farrell (Jackson: University of Mississippi Press, 1992), p. 8.

13.  I. B. Singer, *In My Father's Court* (New York: Fawcett Crest, 1966), p. 148 (*Mayn-tatns-beys-din-shtub* [Tel Aviv: Peretz Farlag, 1979]).

14.  Trans. Maurice Carr (London: Virago, 1983. Rpt. of London: W. and G. Foyle, 1946), p. 7. (*Der sheydim-tants* [Warsaw: Farlag Kh. Bzoza, 1936]). In English, see also Joshua Fogel, "Esther Kreitman and Her Sketch, 'A New World,'" *The Yale Review* 73 (Summer 1984), pp. 525–32.

15.  Clive Sinclair, *The Brothers Singer* (London and New York: Allison and Busby, 1983), p. 122.

16.  (Warsaw: self-publ., 1932).

17.  David G. Roskies, *A Bridge of Longing: The Lost Art of Yiddish Storytelling* (Cambridge, Mass.: Harvard University Press, 1995), p. 103.

18.  See Zamir, p. 30.

19.  Cited in Zamir, p. 32. Nissan is a character in Singer's family saga, *The Brothers Ashkenazi* trans. Maurice Samuel (New York: Knopf, 1936). (*Di brider ashkenazi* [Warsaw: Farlag Kh. Bzoza, 1936]).

20.  Zamir, p. 52.

21.  Trans. Joseph Singer (New York: Funk and Wagnalls, 1969). (*Shtol un ayzn* [Vilna: Kletskin, 1927]). His anti-Stalinism is even more on display in the longer and more successful *Khaver nakhmen* (Comrade Nachman) (New York, 1938); translated by Maurice Samuel as *East of Eden* (New York: A. A. Knopf, 1939).

22.  See Sinclair, *The Brothers Singer*, p. 51. See also Singer's journalistic pieces from his travels in Russia: *Nay Rusland, bilder fun a rayze* (New Russia, images from a voyage) (Vilna: B. Kletskin, 1927).

23.  Ruth Wisse, *The Modern Jewish Canon: A Journey Through Language and Culture* (New York: The Free Press, 2000), p. 139.

24.  Seth Wolitz, "*Di Khalyastre*: The Yiddish Modernist Movement in Poland: An Overview," *Yiddish* 4:3 (1981), p. 6.

25.  See Seth Wolitz, "The Kiev-Grupe (1918–1920) Debate: The Function of Literature," in *Twentieth-Century Eastern European Jewish Culture*, eds. Brian Horowitz and Haim A. Gottshalk (Bloomington: Slavica, 2014), pp. 355–64.

26.  Sol Liptzin, *The Maturing of Yiddish Literature* (New York: Jonathan David Publishers, 1970), p. 145. Seth Wolitz offers a minority opinion that places Singer in the core group ("*Di Khalyastre*," p.15).

27.  Alter Kacyzne and Mikhal Vaykhert, eds., *Ringen*. Kiev and Warsaw: Kultur Lige, 1921. This story was penned in Kiev, 1920.

28.   Gennady Estraikh and Lara Ivry Rabinovitch, "The Old and The New Together: David Bergelson's and Israel Joshua Singer's Portraits of Moscow Circa 1926–27," *Prooftexts* 26: 1–2 (Winter/Spring 2006), pp. 53–78. See also *Nay Rusland.*

29.   I. J. Singer and Perets Markish, eds., *Khalyastre* (Warsaw: Farlag Khalyastre, 1922).

30.   *Khalyastre,* (pp. 21–29).

31.   "Singer [was a] photographic retoucher long before he became . . . [an] author. . . . Kacyzne's studio provided the setting for Singer's very first short story, "In der finsternish." Web, ed. *Poyln: Jewish Life in the Old Country: Alter Kacysne,* "Introduction," p. xv.

32.   Trans. Joseph Singer (New York: Vanguard, 1969) (*Di mishpokhe karnovski.* [New York: Matones, 1943].)

33.   Singer, *Of a World That Is No More*, trans. Joseph Singer (New York: The Vanguard Press, 1970), p. 11 (*Fun a velt vos iz nishto mer* [New York: Matones, 1946]).

34.   Cited in Edward Alexander, *Irving Howe: Socialist, Critic, Jew* (Bloomington: Indiana University Press, 1998), pp. 152–53.

35.   Singer, *Of a World That Is No More*, pp. 29–37.

36.   Wisse, *The Modern Jewish Canon*, p. 138.

37.   Jordan Finkin, *A Rhetorical Conversation: Jewish Discourse in Modern Yiddish Literature* (University Park, Penn.: Pennsylvania State University Press, 2010), pp. 2, 3.

38.   So called in Bashevis's *In My Father's Court*, pp. 197–201.

39.   Cited in Blocker and Elman, "An Interview with Isaac Bashevis Singer," p. 8.

40.   Singer, *Of a World That Is No More*, pp. 21–28.

41.   Singer, *Of a World That Is No More*, p. 237.

42.   Mark Golub, "A Shmues with Isaac Bashevis Singer," in Farrell, ed. *Conversations*, p. 189.

43.   Cited in Liptzin, *The Maturing of Yiddish Literature*, p. 119.

44.   Moyshe Menakhovski, *Gemishte khasenes in der yidisher literatur* (Mixed Marriages in Yiddish literature) (Buenos Aires: YIVO, 1968), pp. 68–70.

45.   Krutikov, *Yiddish Fiction and the Crisis of Modernity, 1905–1914* (Stanford: Stanford University Press, 2001), p. 164.

46.   Norich, *The Homeless Imagination*, p. 60.

47.   Singer, *Of a World That Is No More*, pp. 141, 11.

48.   In Ruth R. Wisse. *A Shtetl and Other Yiddish Novellas* (New York: Behrman House, 1973); original (Warsaw: Progres,1909).

49.  Roskies, *Against the Apocalypse: Responses to Catastrophe in Modern Jewish Culture* (Cambridge, Mass.: Harvard University Press, 1984), p. 113.

50.  *A shtetl* (New York: Forverts, 1911).

51.  Norich, *The Homeless Imagination*, p. 23.

52.  Roskies, *A Bridge of Longing*, pp. 231–32.

53.  Cited in Roskies, *A Bridge of Longing*, p. 232.

54.  Singer, *Of a World That Is No More*, p. 37.

55.  Schwartz acted as the patriarch in both *Yoshe kalb* (1932/1933) and *The Family Carnovsky* (1943) at the Yiddish Art Theater in New York.

56.  Yiddish actor, son of writer Yoysef Opatoshu, appeared in Edgar G. Ulmer's *The Light Ahead*, based on Mendele Moykher *Sforim's Fishke der krumer*.

57.  Singer, *Of a World That Is No More*, p. 37.

# I

# CHAPTER ONE

**A**lthough it was altogether barely a week before Passover, Volf, son of Hirsh Rubin, as yet knew none of the *Song of Songs* traditionally chanted on Passover. The village teacher had been trying since Purim to plow it into his thick skull.

"'I am dark . . .'"—intoned the teacher melodically in Hebrew and then in the Yiddish vernacular: "'So says the congregation of Israel before God—Although I am dark—from sin for I have made the golden calf—but comely. I am beautiful in that I have received the Torah. I am like the tents of Kedar, although I may appear as dark as the tents of the Tatars. As the pavilions of King Solomon, I shall be as white, as luminous as are his drapes'" (*Shir Hashirim* 1:5 with Rashi's Commentary).

Volf merely mimicked his teacher's chanting; when it came to actually pronouncing words on his own, he knew not a single one. The teacher—a slender, pallid man—having spent the entire winter depressed and ensconced in his freshly whitewashed, bluish-tinged, village home, looked at his pupil pityingly.

"Come on, Volf! I beg you, apply yourself," he said in a plaintive voice. "I must return home to my wife and children for Passover. I haven't been home this entire winter. It's your fault! Because you still haven't learned the *Song of Songs*, I haven't been able to go home. . . ."

Volf's chubby, ruddy cheeks, as if wine-stained, became redder still at his teacher's words. His large, black eyes looked at the ashen teacher with compassion. He, at long last, did want to be diligent but the words, singing and strange as they were, just wouldn't sink in: the tents of the

Tatars; the golden calf which the Jews worshipped; King Solomon's white curtains; and the daughters of Jerusalem were all jumbled up in a single cluster—and for the life of him he couldn't crawl out of the tangle.

His father, Reb Hirsh, looked at his son, grown so tall with flushed red cheeks, the likes of which had never been seen among Jewish boys his age. He cast an indignant look at his wife, sitting with a live turkey in her lap which she was force-feeding to fatten it up for Passover.

"I have no idea how it is that I have fathered such a son," he said angrily to his wife, an innkeeper's daughter. "Somehow there is nothing in his face that resembles that of a Jew, this son of yours."

"He's as much yours as he is mine," she replied with resentment, as she clutched the turkey by the throat to force its mouth to open wider so she could stuff more food into it. "And, I don't know why you badger the child as you do."

"The child," repeated Hirsh, mocking his wife's words, "is growing as tall as a gentile. As far as you're concerned, he's still a child, a boy— truth be told—he's more like a cutthroat."

Incensed, he slammed the door and stormed out.

In silence Volf listened patiently to his father's entire speech and his mother's answer, making nothing of both. In one ear and out the other. He abandoned his teacher in the middle of his "rebukes" to the Jewish people who wrestle with their God, and set out for the horse stable, a fair distance off in the yard. At the door he realized that he was hungry, although it hadn't been that long since breakfast. He quickly cut himself a piece of bread—over which one is commanded to recite a blessing—a large, thick slice, shoved it into the pocket of his loose jacket which was always full of flintstone, nails, and broken keys. With his stubby fingers he tore off a piece of bread, placed it between his strong, white teeth, which glinted from between his generous lips, and chewed audibly with eager anticipation.

"Velvl, come back soon," called his mother affectionately after him. "The rebbe still has material to teach you." "I don't want to," said Volf with a mouth full of food. "I'm going to see old Roch in the stable."

"What? Is a horse to be your teacher?" asked his mother. "You're going to learn Torah from him? You're going to grow up to be a peasant!"

"Grow up! You got that right!" countered Volf, aping his mother's insult, even though the *rebbe* always taught him that one should never talk back to one's mother, and that a wayward and stubbornly disobedient son will end up being stoned to death!

He left the house quickly so that no one would be able to catch him as he was leaving.

The land in the expansive yard was still damp from the frost and snow that lasted throughout the winter. Every step left a flat impression in the moisture. Through the errant bits of snow that turned up here and there and the withered leaves that lingered since autumn, fresh blades of grass had pushed their way through, their embarrassed little heads emerging. Randomly, a yellow wildflower had risen precociously early, bereft of its foliage. The hens, sitting on their eggs, were fiercely clucking, not tiring in the least. One particularly resourceful and capable creature was circling widely about with her little chicks, half-featherless still, looking for kernels of corn in the horses' manure, heated by its warmth, while she sternly kept an eye on the yellow cat waiting only for an opportunity to catch a little chick when she, the mother hen, was not protecting it.

"Cluck, cluck, cluck," she, with vociferous rage, warned the cat, from time to time pointing her beak upwards and sharpening her nails, preparing to defend her little ones.

Volf picked up a pebble from the ground and threw it at the cat lying in wait. Like most boys, he hated cats. The cat quickly jumped up on the fence, on whose posts earthenware pots were draining, and peered down at the boy, as if to tease him now that he couldn't catch her. Volf spat at her, bent down to the ground, and lifted up a tiny, weak baby chick, which, aside from a little yellow down, still had no real feathers. The brood's hen was shivering, as she looked warily at Volf, with the very eyes that reassured him that she was not about to spring at him. She saw that he was caressing her little one, calming it in his hands, blowing on it with his warmth, and giving it scraps freshly chewed from his own mouth.

"Here you are, little squealing one, go back to your mother," said Volf to the chick, as he released it tenderly from his hands.

He walked by a dried up, tangled cherry tree, pulled down several withered cherry pits that were still hanging since the summer on a few branches and which had been pecked at by birds, as they looked for a bit of food in their state of withered desiccation. This filled him with joy and strength. He sensed such power in his short, thick fingers that he had a mind to break or damage something. He ran over to a small, young tree to yank it out of the ground, but the tree held on tenaciously by its roots and wouldn't allow itself to be pulled up. So, Volf picked up a rock stuck in the ground and threw it with all his might at a flock of crows that were cawing around a pile of garbage.

"Hey, you damned, vile beasts," he cried in Polish, as was always the case as Jews spoke with animals in a gentile tongue. "Get away, you dark witches, fly way from there! Winter's over!"

The crows flew off with a cacophonous cawing. The birds squawked, danced, played around, chasing one another. The swallows were working diligently under the thatched roofs, searching for the previous year's nests. At the very top of a stack of hay, a stork turned around in full ritual circuits, as in the synagogue on Simchat Torah, and flapped its wings, wanting to disclose nothing and remain where he was. Finally, it leaned its long, thin feet on the top of a pole that jutted out from the hay, and observed the world around it with a certain condescension, like a scout. The sun shone, reflected in every shard of broken glass, on slender branches, on the remaining bits of snow, in every piece of garbage, and on every little brook. With its large wings, the stork smacked the sunny warmth and let out a crazed, high-pitched cry. Volf lifted his eyes and screamed at the stork:

"Your majesty, stork, your nest is on fire!"

In the stork's screeching, Volf felt the great joy of spring, sun, and awakening which had arrived after the long, harsh, freezing days. He took off his cloth hat and threw it in the air several times for joy, though he knew that a Jewish boy ought not stand beneath the heavens with an uncovered head. With a surfeit of energy in all his limbs, he started to run over the soft earth, hurtling quickly ahead until he was back inside the stable.

By a sawed-off tree protruding from the soft ground, there was seated Roch, their old servant who tended the horses; he was whittling a branch with a knife.

"What're you up to, Roch?" asked Volf of the old man.

The gentile slipped off his filthy peasant shirt—which had been fastened with a small, red, glass button—from his wrinkled, brown, veined neck. With joy did he smooth out all the creases in his skinny, bony face which resembled the bark of an old tree, revealing the huge, one-and-only yellow tooth in his otherwise toothless grin.

"I'm making a pipe for myself, Volf," he said with pride, his squint of delight highlighting all the folds surrounding his small, green eyes. "I broke off a little branch of a cherry tree and ruined it. No need to tell your father. The best pipes are made from the wood of cherry trees."

"I'm not going to tell him, Roch," Volf promised. "But, where's your old pipe?"

"The old one? I sold it to a gypsy. It brought in good money. A half ruble in silver."

Volf sat down on the pile of withered leaves next to old Roch and watched as he deftly whittled away at the hard wood with his knife. The old man did not stop talking in his frail, elderly voice, beaming gleefully with his singular, pointed tooth. His story about the pipe that he sold to the gypsies for half a silver ruble had made him very happy indeed.

"Gypsies fiercely love their old pipes, Volf," he murmured, "but not for smoking—only for eating. They crack the shank of the pipe, scrape off the black sediment that collects there from smoking tobacco, and then they eat it."

Volf grimaced.

"Ugh, what pigs! It doesn't cause them any harm?

"No, they only get healthier as a result," said Roch. "Even their wives delight in this, as if it were whisky."

Volf spat out at the gypsies who gobbled up such an abomination and went into the stable to their horses.

The horses were already in the field. The servants plowed the fields to sow summer corn and to plant potatoes. Only the pregnant mares, no longer able to plow, remained in the stable, where they were likely to give birth to colts, on any given day. Shuffling about with their full, rounded bellies, they lazily picked at the hay by the trough with the ladder on top. Lying on the ground, after labor, was a young brown-haired horse, licking its newborn foal, as a mother shows tenderness to its child, applying its red cheek to the soft hide of the young one.

"Are you going to give this one a name, Volf?" asked old Roch, still carving his pipe.

"I've been thinking about it all night and haven't come up with anything yet," said Volf. "Hand me a bit of salt, Roch, so I can salt the little one. Kasha's already licked up all the salt we gave it."

Roch climbed up to the slightly rotting roof spars where the salt was kept, and he handed some to the boy. Just as his mother would salt meat before cooking, Volf rubbed it on the young creature, who was weakly trying to stand up on its faltering, spindly little legs.

The mare soon turned to lick up the salt on her newborn.

"The more it licks the salt, the better it washes the newborn," said Volf happily, his fingers petting the short bristly hair on the foal's pliant neck.

He loved all the animals in the yard. What is more, he knew and understood all the fowl, the cows and their calves. And had no fear of the irascible bull, which was always attached by a chain to the trough and separated from all the cows; Volf stroked its mighty neck. But, more than all the others, even the dogs, he loved the horses, especially the colts. He always had to be in the stable when a mare was giving birth to aid old Roch in delivering the newborns.

His father used to beat him for this, because a boy wasn't supposed to mix with animals or pay attention to such things. That was old Roch's affair. But all the slaps in the world had no effect. Volf always stood in the stable during the first days of spring when the animals gave birth. Nothing could deter him from attending to the horses.

"The boy is going to grow up to be a horses' groom or a wagon-driver," predicted the father. "God grant that my words not come true."

No, Reb Hirsh Rubin was not terribly pleased with Volf. Although he was a village Jew, the owner of a substantial farm, he nonetheless had no love for the inn that he had inherited from his father-in-law, the innkeeper.

Reb Hirsh had been a city man, an assiduous student; because of this his father-in-law had accepted him as a son-in-law for his only daughter and gave him his entire estate—numerous fields, gardens, orchards, that is, an estate replete with buildings, cows, horses, fowl, barns, and stables. After his father-in-law's death, he remained in the village, lord of the estate, although he could never get used to it. The work of the farm was performed by the peasants and servants, as well as his wife who had become accustomed to such work.

Reb Hirsh couldn't so much as hitch up a horse—he was afraid even to approach one. Although his dogs ran after him and licked him, he had little confidence in them, and secretly he was even a bit afraid of them.

"You can't trust a dog," he mumbled, chasing away the dogs that ran after him with their outstretched necks, longing for a caress.

He couldn't bear the peasants with their rough-sounding speech, the stench of their foul-smelling pipes, their crude laughter, their boorishness. He thus often went to visit his rebbe, although he was certainly no fervent Hasid, and he'd sit there every trip for weeks at a time, if only to be among Jews, to speak about Torah and business affairs, and to hear stories and anecdotes about wars that might come their way. The authors of religious works who traveled around—men looking for book subscriptions, those who lost everything in fires, preachers, beautiful impoverished Jews, paupers—all would drop in to see Reb Hirsh in the village and sit with him for a few days, even weeks, at his expense. Reb Hirsh truly enjoyed himself with these Jews, sitting with them for hours at a time at the table, listening to their stories and discussing the old days at great length. They would all leave with plenty of alms; they were well-fed on rich milk, butter, eggs, and chicken broth.

During the winter months when the roads were covered with snow and no outsiders came to the village, Reb Hirsh wandered around aimlessly like a lost soul. He chewed his beard in resentment and cracked his knuckles nervously, so that people everywhere could hear them breaking. He then looked up at the whitewashed rafters.

"Master of the universe, deliver me from this village," he begged, "and bring me to be among Jews."

It was his constant wish that he might sell the estate, turn it over for half its value, and move to a city with Jewish people.

But he never found a buyer. Just as he had no desire to have contact with these gentile pursuits, he tried to guard against his sons' doing the same. He hired an itinerant teacher for them and saw that they studied Torah with Rashi's commentary, Talmud, and accounting. Should one of them wish to approach a horse, he would scold them:

"Don't touch the animals. You'll forget what you've studied."

The only one who could not pull himself away from the gentiles and the animals was Volf. From childhood on, this lad had no head for Torah and demonstrated behavior that filled Reb Hirsh with fear. Volf would place his hand deep into the jagged-toothed mouths of the largest dogs, having no worries whatsoever about being bitten. He rolled around with the dogs on the ground. He caught birds and tamed them. In wintertime, when a half-frozen bird would beat its wings on the frosty windowpane, he'd let it in, allow it to warm up, breathe into its beak for a long time with his own steamy breath until it was revived and made healthy again. He was also able to bind the foot of a bleeding dog whose bone had been bitten into by a much stronger dog in a fight over a female. In the event that someone else's cow wandered into their fields, he would not abandon it until he'd "taken it by the horns" and led it to the stable, and he'd hold onto it until the owner came with a *złoty* to redeem it for the harm it caused.

Reb Hirsh scolded him:

"Listen here, boy, I don't want to get involved with gentiles, so get rid of the cow."

But Volf chose not to hear him:

"Why? If one of our animals wandered off to their fields, they'll take it in and demand a reward to get it back," said Volf passionately. "Our fields aren't ownerless either."

No riff-raff scared him, as he always stood in total preparedness, summoning his physical prowess to fight off anyone who laid a hand on him. His heart and mind were trained exclusively on the horses. He rode the strongest horse without a bridle, simply by holding on to its mane. He would crawl down under the horse's abdomen and clean away any manure or filth with an iron comb. If a young, unshod horse were to have a glass splinter in its foot, or a small nail in its hoof, he would lift the horse's wounded foot, place it on his knee, and treat and bind it for as long as needed until the patient was cured. He fettered the most malicious horse by its front legs, so that it wouldn't be able to stray too far into the pasture; he also counted the number of teeth in the mouths of the wild stallions to establish how old they were. More than anything, he felt attached to the colts, to the young, little horses. Entire days he would run around with them in the meadow, taking care of them lest they embark prematurely on a love affair; he did not let any of the village youths climb up and ride them, because that would impede the younger horses as they grew.

Volf received going away presents from passing merchants, and Hanukkah presents from his mother. Every penny he would put toward the purchase of a colt from a peasant. Before anyone looked around and paid heed, he was raising another young, spoiled and demanding horse. He would even bring the colts into his home to give them some sugar to snack on.

His father would scream at him, smack him, and bemoan the fact that this youngster would grow up to be a gentile. But Volf would never be deterred from caring for his horses. So, he'd leave his teacher's Torah behind, and off he'd go to the meadow.

"Reb Hirsh," lamented the tutor, "to take the pay you've given me to teach the boy would be a sin. I'm not his teacher—that old gentile is."

"Beat him, break his bones," Reb Hirsh implored him: "I beg of you!" "Who has the strength?" answered the tutor in humiliation. "I thank God that he hasn't hit me. Someone that strong!"

Reb Hirsh looked downcast and grumbled irately in the direction of his wife, the innkeeper's daughter, who took the boy's side:

"His mother's son," he murmured into his beard. "It's hopeless."

**2**

# CHAPTER TWO

**W**hen Volf turned twenty-one years of age and after *Sukkoth* (Feast of Tabernacles) had to take up his military duty, Reb Hirsh wanted to sell several acres of land and a couple of animals so that he might use the money to redeem his son from gentile hands. Volf refused entrance to any peasant who came to speak with his father about buying land.

"Go with God!" he goaded the buyers to leave, "we're not selling."

His father tried to knock some sense into him:

"No sooner will you be discharged, thick head, then you'll be presented with good matches with dowries, and we'll get back our investments with more than we started."

Volf did not want to hear about it. Like all the young ruffians of the village who'd turned twenty-one years of age, he set to stitching himself a pair of good boots, making a box from odd boards to pack his things, painted it green, and bought himself a hood as well as a sheepskin hat. And, just like all the other youngsters in the village, he made his way to the city to present himself before the doctors and officers who selected men to serve in the Tsar's army.

"Your name and surname?" asked a plump man with a red beard, the head functionary, to the naked, grown up young man.

"Volf Rubin," answered the unclothed youth.

"Employment?"

"A farmer."

"Healthy?"

"Healthy!"

The official used his fat hand to rub first one eye and then the other, and then, with his eyes wide open then wiped dry, stared incredulously at the naked youngster.

"A Jew?" he asked in utter amazement.

"A Jew!" answered the naked lad.

The plump man turned around to the doctors and the military men and called out:

"Gentlemen, come look at something extraordinary. A Jew, a farmer, who says he's healthy."

Everyone walked over to where the naked young man stood and skeptically looked him up and down.

There stood Volf Rubin, among all the young men of the town who were bespectacled, emaciated, in pain from fasting and eating only herring, so as to make themselves thin. Among the bookish ones living off their in-laws, there were those who heard a ringing in their ears, whose feet were missing a toe and who were toothless, or had a hernia at the tender age of twenty-one. In a huddle of frightened, naked, bent-over young men, the best bodies standing there hapless with limp hands and feet, intentionally, so as not to find favor with the senior official with their golden epaulets—among all of these pretenders to physical impairment—there stood Volf Rubin, stiffly erect and proud of his strength, yet cautiously circumspect.

"Healthy!" he replied in a loud voice and in Slavic tones to all of the questions put to him by the doctor.

The military men were delighted.

"Well-built!" the doctor praised him. "Broad-shouldered and narrow- waisted, clear eyes, teeth all in place."

"And with such a long stride," murmured the officer as he moved his hand over the young man's strong, well-turned feet. "He'll be ideal for the cavalry."

"Passed!" called out the older official loudly as he gave the recruit a smack on the behind, as one might thwack a horse that one was purchasing on his hind-quarters.

For the next four weeks until he was turned over to his regiment, Volf put the family stable in order. He mended the bridles, patched up the horses' collars, brushed and adorned them, and washed them down, all the while pressing his face affectionately against their necks and heads.

"Father, you mustn't sell them. Do you hear me?" he beseeched his father every day. "These few years of service will fly by, and I'll be back at work, applying myself diligently. But, you can't sell them, Father!"

"If only he would miss his mother and father as much as he does the horses," said Reb Hirsh resentfully.

Of all the recruits and especially the Jews, it was Volf Rubin whom the non-commissioned officer, the riding instructor, chose to deride.

"When you sit on a horse, you face its head, not its tail," he said to Volf with contrived earnestness. "And when the horse runs, you don't scream out: 'Mommy, Daddy,' but hold firm in the saddle. You understand?"

Volf was not fazed but silently listened to the gentile's jokes. At first the non-commissioned officer let him ride around slowly in the circular riding area. On one occasion he cracked his whip at the horse's feet and laughed loudly to the older cavalrymen:

"Watch it soar," he prophesied, "ha, ha."

But Volf tightened his grasp on the reins in anticipation of the raucous ride and braced his knees against the horse's sides. Used to inept recruits, the horse reared up on its hind legs to throw off its obstinate rider. Volf remained firmly in the saddle. The horse tried to kick. It lowered its head as if surrendering, and then suddenly lowered its front legs and with the rear ones leapt precipitously into the air to throw the rider in front up over its head. Volf surmised the horse's ploy in advance and would not allow it to fling him from the saddle. The horse then lowered his slender neck, with piercing intelligence looked the rider up and down, and surrendered. The non-commissioned officer remained in place, mouth agape and head cocked haughtily.

"You're some kind of clever fellow, aren't you?" he said with both regret and respect. "Good, you'll teach the other recruits how to ride."

Military service for Volf went smoothly, without obstacle or hindrance. He was an excellent rider, an accurate shot, a skillful fencer and a nimble jumper. He knew by heart military law with all the titles of the Tsar and the members of the elite. At every military inspection, when a general appeared and they had to present the best soldier, Volf was always selected. After the first year he received a ribbon—a little later, another one. For his exceptional shooting, he was given a cheap, huge pocket-watch with an inscription. He would have received a third ribbon, but no one would ever give a Jew more than two ribbons. The letters he wrote home were never mournful, like most of the letters of Jewish soldiers. Together with greetings to his parents, sisters and brothers, he sent greetings to every single horse and colt, every cow and calf, inquiring about the well-being of each animal and concluding with his constant plea:

"Father, sell nothing of the household, nothing. Let me return from the Russki army, and I will get right to work on it."

After three years and eight months of service, Volf returned home, all dressed up in the new military uniform of a cavalryman with buttons, Russian army stripes along the sides of his trousers, and his two ribbons. He was whipped by sun and wind, sunburnt, strong, and very happy. His whiskers, rakishly cut, had sprouted, so that Volf exuded masculinity and charm. But the old, familiar estate was no longer in his parents' possession. Strangers had taken up residence. His parents were living in a neighboring town, a very small one at that, a cramped, gloomy, garbage-strewn place. Among all the merchants was his father sitting in his own dark dry goods store and looking at the wares that were scattered here and there in open drawers, as he rather patiently waited for a customer who would never appear.

"Why did you sell it?" asked an embittered Volf. "I begged you not to sell!"

"I couldn't stand it any longer in the village," said his father. "I wanted to be a Jew among Jews."

Volf set out to take a close and detailed look at the town. From every little shop, through windows and doorways, heads poked out with curiosity. The girls were fiercely attracted to him. Elementary school boys ran after him and stared in wonderment and surprise at his cavalryman's uniform as well as the ribbons on his epaulets. The policeman in the market greeted him with a military flourish.

For several weeks he walked around exclusively in his military clothing. His father chastised him:

"Volf, get out of the Russki army garments! Get back into clothes that befit a Jew. I'm publicly mortified."

Volf made no reply. Matchmakers began to beat a path to Reb Hirsh's threshold in the shop to effect matches for Volf. The fathers of girls of marriageable age began to address the serious and practical issue of finding partners for them. Volf remained silent. He would go out all day, walk on foot to their farms, investigate the earth, the buildings, the horses in the meadows, and then return home embittered. On many an occasion he would lie down for an entire twenty-four-hour period and sleep away the whole day and night. After a few weeks of silence and ambling about, he took off his military garb and sold it for whatever he could get. He also sold the oversized pocket watch that he'd gotten as a gift for accuracy in shooting. Packing up a little laundry, a needle and thread, and a few other things that a man needs on the road into his green military box, he just took off one day for the frontier and, without so much as a "farewell," stole across the border into Galicia. The moment he was on the other side, he wrote a picture postcard home:

"Dear Mother and Father," he wrote on the postcard which bore a picture of Emperor Franz Joseph in full imperial splendor, "I'm off to the United States to start a new and different life. When I reach my destination, wherever it may be, I'll write."

**3**

# CHAPTER THREE

As was the case several years previously when he was in the military, so was it now on board ship anchored in New York harbor: Volf Rubin, the immigrant, was the exception among the teeming mass of Jews lined up in a row before a quarantine doctor who was examining them.

The rocking back and forth for several weeks all the way from Hamburg to New York on the very tip of the bow of an old ship did not viscerally unnerve Volf, as it did most of his fellow passengers. Used as he was to riding horses, the ship's pitching had no effect on him whatsoever. He was continually walking around the deck, observing the sailors at work; his face was scorched by the sun and lashed by the winds and storms. Every time that the deck sailor sounded the signal for eating, he would quickly take down from the wall a small kettle with a spoon that hung from a nail over his bed and made his way to the cook with the smoke-blackened white chef's cap on his thick, perfectly round head.

The food was plentiful. Most of the passengers became sick and couldn't eat a single morsel of food. The observant Jews, ravenous, wouldn't so much as taste the non-kosher food; they also suffered from dehydration. The cook would thus generously fill Volf's kettle to the brim, shuffle off toward him large portions of meat, and also slip him more than enough bread. Volf ate with a soldier's appetite and helped the sailors with their efforts at summoning his physical prowess. The observant Jews, pallid and ailing, as if at the end of a fast, interrupted their reciting of Psalms to watch the young man as he chewed the non-kosher fare with great gusto and sent quiet sighs in his direction:

"He hasn't even reached the shore and already he's eating non-kosher food," they murmured to one another and, after smacking their lips, returned to reciting Psalms, beseeching God to protect the listing ship from the menacing, swiftly undulating waves.

Among all the pale, sickly, dejected people lined up before the quarantine doctor, Volf—ruddy-cheeked, sun-tanned, robust, and fresh—shone with all the charms and vigor of youth.

*"Ein Jude?"* asked the clerk in the green uniform in German, as he looked at the papers in astonishment at the man's attestation of his employment.

"A Jew," replied Volf, expressing himself in the drawn-out, slow talk as was a soldier's fashion, whenever he saw a uniform with buttons standing before him.

The doctor didn't even examine him properly; he glanced at Volf's dark eyes which beamed out from his bronzed face and at the fingers of his strong hands, and he gave Volf a clap on the back, happily winking at him. And just like that, the man in the white coat smiled at Volf and inoculated him against smallpox.

*"Gute Muskeln,"* he commended Volf for his strength, as his steady hand guided the needle for the injection. "We need arms like that in America."

Volf stepped down, with his green soldier's box, onto this new land, ready to make use of the muscular hands that he would need in America. But no one seized the opportunity to utilize his hands for what he was capable of doing. Together with the pallid little Jews, he was led to a crowded street, above which an elevated railway passed by, making an overhead racket. Like others, he was then placed in a packed absorption center, given food, and registered for work with a rather small, Galician Jew who spoke Yiddish with a healthy admixture of Germanisms and who needed men to make cigars. In a large hall with windows covered with dust and iron bars, through which not the slightest ray of sunlight or air entered, sat men and women at long tables, withered, pale, with weary eyes and frail bodies, deeply engrossed in the tobacco's brown leaves, coughing all the while from the dust and the arduousness of the labor.

"Where's your home?" asked the little Jew of the tall, grown-up young man as he looked up at him, looming above.

Volf didn't understand the language he was using.

"Where are you from in Russia, where? That's what I'm asking you," he asked, switching from German to Galician Yiddish.

"I worked on the land," said Volf. "I'm from a village."

"Hmm. . . . A peasant," he said with a smile on his face. "Sit down at the table and do what everyone else is doing, only do it quickly! You've got—may there be no evil eye—a pair of powerful hands, like a *goy*."

Volf took a seat at the table to get to work, but his hands, for all their might and dexterity, were not adept at all when handling the brown tobacco leaves. He constantly tore the fine leaves in his rough hands. While he was the laughing stock of his fellow workers, the boss consoled him:

"Every beginning is hard, as the Talmudists say, but pay it no heed. You'll get better at it with time. It'll become a habit."

But Volf didn't quite get the hang of it. The thin leaves all split and cracked as soon as he laid hands on them. After several days, the boss gave him his marching papers.

"You've got the mind of a peasant," he scolded Volf. "It's not made for a delicate line of work like this."

At the shelter, they sent him to another site to work, a tailor's shop, to stitch buttons on pants. But, there too Volf's hands were ill-fit for the work. The needle vanished from among his clumsy, rough fingers. It went terribly slowly, as if he were working with pitch.

"With stitching like that, you'll earn water on your kasha, or next to nothing," said the master craftsman to him. "You're working at a snail's pace, like molasses in January. . . . Look here at how others are doing it."

He led Volf over to a small-boned, slender girl who was manipulating the needle in her pale fingers with wild abandon and speed; she was to teach him how to do it properly.

"Take a look—as small as she is, she is able to make a lot of money. Study this and take it in!

But he couldn't learn. His fingers just wouldn't cooperate. His hands which could so nimbly handle an ax and a plough, a horse's reins, and a soldier's rifle were thoroughly useless when it came to a needle and thread, unfit for this boring, lesser women's work. He didn't stay long at any job. He went from sweatshop to sweatshop, from stitching buttons to sewing with white basting thread, from attaching hooks to embroidering holes. Volf couldn't master any of these skills. This earned him the ridicule of the girls and the mockery of the gifted tailors.

One hot night during a heat wave, when the flies and bedbugs were stubbornly gnawing on the sweaty bodies of the people in their suffocating little rooms, and the elevated trains refused to stop rattling in their tired, fevered heads, Volf took his mattress to the roof and laid down among numerous other mattresses that were arranged and crowded with men, women, and children. It was a bright, starry night. The moon which Volf had not seen for so long in the crowded, dense city peered down at him, a familiar and close force of nature, just as it was in the village, when he tended the horses in the evening, and just like it was among the soldiers when he would stand on guard at night. At times like these, his homesickness caught up with him. He lit a cigarette and whistled a shepherd's tune that he remembered from the time when he would whistle through a branch in the village.

From a nearby mattress, a person raised his unkempt head of hair and cleared his throat several times.

"You miss home?" asked the disheveled person with a dry, shrill Litvak accent, yawning into the night.

Volf didn't reply and just kept on whistling.

The man lifted his filthy pillow, grabbed a tobacco pouch, and rolled a cigarette. He nervously blew thick and hurried rings of smoke from his mouth and nose, coughed dryly, and spoke again to Volf, though the latter had not replied the first time.

"Such a pair of hands, it's a sin to waste them in a sweatshop, young man," he said and looked sullenly at Volf's powerful, half-naked body.

Volf stopped whistling.

"What do you mean?" he asked the disheveled man.

The man cleared his throat of the harsh smoke on which he was choking and proceeded to bombard Volf with questions one after the next:

"Can you carry a heavy load?"

"I can," answered Volf suspiciously, not knowing what the Litvak was aiming at.

Like every Polish Jew, he suspected that the Litvak wanted to cheat him.

"Can you move on your feet?"

"I can."

"Do you like women?"

"Yeah, so?"

"You're crazy to stay in New York," he said, "when you can travel far and wide and peddle to the farmers. You will accumulate great wealth, perhaps even a substantial estate, and the women farmers will fall madly in love with you! Mark my words!"

Volf looked at the man with a penetrating stare and remained silent. The man cleared his throat of cigarette smoke very loudly and spoke with fervor and conviction:

"Spit on New York," he said. "Come with me. We'll go from farm to farm, from city to city. In just a few years, we'll have a real business. All of them began as peddlers. Now, they're fabulously wealthy, as rich as Croesus!"

Volf lit a fresh cigarette and considered the matter. From what the Litvak had to say, enveloped in smoke and coughing, he was thrilled by the heady promise of traveling over villages, over fields and forests, being free, not suffocating in crowded sweatshops, not engaged in women's work. The mere thought of this sent a mild wind blowing from his toes to the hair on his head.

"Okay," he said, "but I'm no good at business. I've never done it."

"You'll learn the art of it," said the coughing man derisively.

"And, I can't utter a single English word."

"You'll soon familiarize yourself with the few words you need. Incidentally, leave the speaking to me. You just help me carry packages, shoo dogs away when they attack, smack those smart alecks if they bother us along the road. Can you do all that?"

"Well, just let someone try something!" said Volf making a fist.

"When we make the first few dollars, we'll buy a horse and a little wagon to travel in. You know your way around a horse?"

The man's question so made Volf want to laugh out loud that he couldn't hold himself back.

"Do I know how to handle a horse?" he asked with joy. "Man, what are you talking about?"

The coughing man tapped the ash from his cigarette and extended a bony and greedy hand to Volf.

"Are we off then?"

"It's a deal!" said Volf, pressing the man's thin hand in his own warm, tenacious grasp. He was ready to go to the end of the world as long as he could have a horse by his side.

**4**

# CHAPTER FOUR

**A**s an animal bursts out of its cage, so too did Volf Rubin, with great exuberance and joy, tear himself away from the gritty, smoky city onto the open road in the great, free outdoors replete with meadows, fields, and rivers. He was carrying two bundles of wares: one his own behind him attached to his shoulders with straps, and one in front belonging to his partner. The Litvak groaned under the weight of his bundle, coughing up thick phlegm, so Volf took it and hoisted it on himself. Yet he felt he wasn't burdened at all. His large, strong legs in broad, velvet trousers strode along with an ample military step.

"Don't run like that. I can't keep up with you," beseeched his partner, coughing.

Volf slackened his stride, and then soon forgot about his travelling companion and lurched ahead, leaving him a way's behind.

With flaring nostrils, he smelled the pure air, inhaled the aroma of the grass, the grain, the flowers in the field, and the water; he sensed such strength in his hands that it aroused in him a strong desire to accomplish something. Every few hours he'd untie his bundle, take out some bread and cheese, several bananas, a flask of water and eat ravenously, throwing the crumbs to the birds congregated around his feet, detecting food.

"Eat. You need strength for the trip," he said to his partner.

"I'm better off smoking," replied the Litvak as he rolled another cigarette with the tip of his yellow fingers which were always fiddling with tobacco.

He smoked more than ate, cleared his throat and hacked dryly and persistently.

For as long as they were on the road, Volf was above and his partner below. Although a foreigner in the country, and a newcomer to the countryside, Volf nonetheless became acquainted with the land, made his way along the road well, detecting rural paths and trails with proficiency. Dogs would not bark at him, as if in him they sensed a friend and stretched out their necks to be petted. All this time, he taught his coughing partner the secrets of fields and woods: what kind of rye in summertime and what in wintertime; what kind of earth is black and what is sandy; what kind of leaves came from cabbage and what from potatoes. He cited all the names of grasses and flowers, of trees and mushrooms. At every field they passed, he yanked off an ear of corn, chewed it and, with a peasant's joy, beamed with the satisfaction that this appeared to be an abundant harvest. His smoking partner listened silently and sucked with great effort on the last little stub of his cigarette with the fire perilously close to his lips. He had nothing to add to Volf's worldly wise speech.

Whenever they would approach a farmhouse and knock on the door, the coughing partner appeared twice his normal size, while Volf bowed his head in humility and deference. Soon after the first time, his partner set out for one house and sent him with a bundle to another. Volf just stood there bewildered, like a child abandoned by its mother. He knocked meekly on the farmhouse door. From within, a tall farmer came out and angrily scrutinized his peddler's bundle.

"No peddlers!" he roared in English.

Volf turned red; the blood in his body rushed to his face.

"Good stuff, sir," Volf said praising his own merchandise, as his partner taught him to say: "bargains."

"Get out of here!" the lanky farmer began to shout. "Get out!"

Volf ran off, as if driven away with a whip.

When his partner came over to ask what he had sold, Volf threw his bundle at his feet.

"I don't want any more of this!" he cried out. "I'm done with it."

The partner laughed out loud at him:

"What's this? Your Polish sense of honor is offended?"

Volf remained quiet, miserable, while his partner sat down next to him for a moment on the grass.

"You're a novice at this," he said to Volf. "When a farmer says he's not going to buy anything, pay him no mind and you sell him something anyway. All farmers say the same thing, and all of them will buy later."

Volf wanted to dismiss the whole affair; he did not want to deal with it.

"He screamed at me as if I were a beggar," Volf explained earnestly: "Get out, get out!"

"Ha, ha, ha!" laughed his partner. "So, he told you to get out! You think this is the first time this has ever happened? I'll show you that I'll do business with him yet!"

Volf grabbed his partner by the hand: "Don't go there. He'll slam the door right on your nose!"

"I have a piece of advice in that case," said the partner. "As soon as someone opens the door for me, I stick my foot preemptively inside, and if I can keep my foot in the doorway, no one can close it shut."

With a leisurely gait, bent over toward the ground under his bundle, the partner walked up to the farmer's door, disappearing there for a short time.

Volf sat there restlessly. He thought that something untoward must have happened to the man to make him tarry so long; he wanted to snatch a peek to see if he ought not offer a helping hand. His helping hand, however, was not needed. His partner came out of the house with a straighter back and a lighter bundle. His ordinarily dark face was glowing.

"*Nu*, didn't I tell you?" he said triumphantly. "Such a beautiful few dollars taken in, and deservedly so! May we have as many good, healthy years for the bounty and profits gained in every quarter."

He snapped the fresh, new banknotes in his skinny fingers.

Throughout his long journey over highways and byways, the coughing man never stopped instilling in Volf a peddler's wisdom. He taught him how to argue with a farmer and how to address and sweet talk a farmer's wife. He recounted to him all his tricks and new ideas to entice a customer, how to negotiate a price, how to pacify an irascible person with appropriate words, how to offer advice for all the worries that a farmer might have. Volf listened attentively and nodded his assent:

"Great, great, I'll do just that."

But, no sooner did he approach a door and was met by the greeting, "no peddlers," than he was quickly dispatched. Nor could he propose any inflated prices and then come down by half, no haggling and swearing, and most definitely no confidential or flattering talk. His partner was simply unable to turn him into a respectable and responsible adult.

"He's a knucklehead," he complained to other peddlers when he'd meet them in the cities in kosher cafes.

"He wasn't put on this earth to be a peddler," the other peddlers prophesied, playing cards at their tables.

Volf said nothing. He found he had no place among the peddlers who arrived at the restaurant in large groups. They laughed, boasted of their good fortune, recounted their brilliant notions and fresh ideas. The younger men told of miracles concerning the women who fell in love with them in the villages where they spent the night. Some of them counted out their dollars and calculated when they'd be able to accumulate enough money for a ship's ticket to bring their wives and children from far off on the other side of the sea. These practical Jews noted in their bankbooks their savings written clearly in columns just like soldiers on review. With lead pencils, they took stock of their bills, cash, and debts, and, what is more, they counted on their fingers the number of months they still had to traipse around with their bundles. Only then would they have sufficient money to be able to open a little store in a gentile town where businesses had not yet been pillaged through rivalries and competition.

People were smoking, playing, telling stories, bragging, cursing, scoffing, rebuking, kibitzing, making deals, each sticking his nose in the other fellow's business, while callously touching a nerve. Volf had nothing to say to them. He left by the door, with a few pieces of bread in his pocket, whistling to the birds which flocked around his feet in search of crumbs.

"I am anxious to know what he will jeer at next," said his partner to the men at the small tables, "so he whistles and is silent like a stranger."

"In any case, no bankbook there," murmured several of the men into their beards. "A peddler has to know how to fool his customers, not how to jeer at them. He won't be carrying his bundle around for much longer. You'll see!"

Their words quickly proved to be true. Just as Volf had unexpectedly fallen in with these Jews with their bundles, he just as unexpectedly dropped out.

On a subsequent summer evening, they—both partners—came upon a secluded farm and knocked on the door to see if they might spend the night there. The farm was located at a site isolated from its surroundings. The house was old and eerily unsettling. No one opened the door in response. They walked away toward the yard, and at the well located there in the middle of the yard a horse, in agony, lay kicking the earth with his hooves. Nearby stood an old farmer with rolled-up sleeves, silently staring, with a dark and concerned gaze, at the sickly horse.

"Good evening, sir," Volf's partner said in English to the man by the horse.

The farmer made no reply. He glanced with his bright blue eyes at the two of them with their bundles, spat with disdain at the ground, and with a twisted mouth, muttered:

"No business here, strangers!" he said angrily and looked back at the horse clattering its hooves on the ground.

Volf's partner wanted to relieve the farmer's sorrow, and a smile came across his downcast face.

"Can we help you in some way?" he asked obsequiously.

The farmer glared at him icily.

"You're an idiot!" he roared in anger.

All the disdain a villager has for a city dweller—a cosmopolitan who is skillful only in conversation and not in practical matters such as helping a suffering horse—was reflected in the farmer's clear blue eyes. He stared at the man with the bundle who didn't understand that under such sad circumstances, one should just keep quiet and leave a man in peace.

The peddler coughed dryly and gloomily. He saw clearly now that he had barged in at a bad time, and he began to tug at Volf by the hem of his jacket.

"Come, Volf, we'll have to look for another farm. It's getting late."

Volf lowered his bundle from his shoulders and off his jacket; silently he bent down to the horse and wiped away the saliva around its mouth with a bit of hay that was lying nearby. He then skillfully pried open the horse's lips, so that he bared all its teeth. In Volf's gentle approach to the horse, the farmer noticed his competence and cordiality.

"What's the trouble?" he asked in English, the very words his partner had taught him to say when a buyer complained about some commodity or other. The farmer was no longer as furious as he had been before. He eyed the strange young man for a while and slowly explained his plight. The horse was perfectly healthy and strong, grazing in the meadow. Suddenly, it was overcome and began to kick. On top of this, the farmer was all alone. His daughter was off in the town, and the horse doctor lived far away, several dozen miles. Such a good, strong horse.

Volf understood very little of the farmer's English, which, to add insult to injury, sounded muffled, because not for a single instant did he remove the pipe from his mouth. But, given the horse's muscle tremors and the smacking of its tail on the ground, he saw that it had eaten too much of something and was suffering from stomach cramps. He was an expert at such things. More than once had he confronted such a case in which a horse threw itself with such abandon to a field of oats, or even to a bucket of dry, unadulterated oats; he then succumbed to bowel upset and stretched out its limbs to its very hooves. The horse had to purge its stomach promptly.

"Ask him if the horse wasn't recently wallowing in oats," said Volf to his partner.

"You ask him!" the Litvak said angrily. "It's good to ask when you can. How the devil do I know the word for 'oats' in English?"

So, Volf tried to communicate with the farmer in sign language.

He walked over to the stable, grabbed some oats, and pointed out the fields to the farmer. He then brought the oats over to the horse's mouth; the horse started to chomp hastily. Like a bolt from the blue, the farmer's eyes opened wide with astonishment.

"That's right!" he said.

Volf rolled up the sleeves of his shirt and quickly set to rescuing the horse. He selected a rope from the stable and tied up the horse's hooves with it, both front and back, so that they wouldn't move away. Then he directed the farmer to boil some water—a lot of water—in the biggest pot he had, and then to hand him the water with soap and everything else that was needed. The farmer executed every step with youthful alacrity. Volf instructed the old man about what he needed to do to the horse, including firmly holding its head; he then placed the horse's tail in his partner's hands.

"Hold tight!" he ordered. "Don't let go!"

They carried out his commands. Volf sat down and sprayed the horse with fluid into its bowels.

"Hold tight! Hold tight! he said, rebuking his partner who was holding the horse's tail with a lack of strength, out of fear.

The horse's flanks became fuller and fuller with each spray of water. Volf untied the gasping horse's legs and washed his own hands off at the well.

"Let the horse lie as it is," he urged them. "It'll start feeling better soon."

With the serenity of a doctor who had successfully completed his work, he wiped his damp hands in some hay and took from his bundle his bread and cheese for supper.

Soon, just as he had predicted, the sick horse began to defecate where it stood, in fact to excrete so voluminously that its flanks kept losing more and more bulk. Shortly thereafter, it got up on its knees, testing their own strength to see if they'd hold it up and get it off the ground, all the while sneezing any number of times. By itself, without another word directed at it, the horse walked back inside the stable.

The farmer brought a cup of milk from his house and placed it before Volf.

"God bless you, stranger!" he said to Volf in English and shook his hand. "You'll spend the night in the house with me. My daughter will soon be returning, and she'll make up a place for you to sleep."

With his pipe in his mouth, spitting here and there, the farmer sat down beside Volf and lethargically questioned him about where he came from, what was his line of work at home and from which village he hails. Volf offered his answers through his partner who relayed them in his citified English. The coughing partner conveyed in his own idiom a far more evocative world than Volf's simple, unsophisticated words could express. He explained to the farmer the wonders of New York where bridges are suspended over rivers, the rail lines that run right down the middle of the street in the air, the skyscrapers, the banks and businesses, the ships that arrive in port, and the flying fish one sees in the sea when one travels over it. The pupils in the farmer's blue eyes doubled in size in utter surprise.

"Such nice things," said the villager in praise, suspending his astonishment to inhale the tobacco in his pipe.

A fair bit of time later, a wagon drove up, a farmer's buggy with a single horse harnessed to it.

"My daughter, Esther," said the farmer and walked over to the door to tell her about the sick horse and the strangers whom God sent in the nick of time.

"That's the guy," he said in English, pointing out Volf, "a nice young man."

The woman who had just arrived was as thin and dried up as her father, with masculine hands and feet and a flat bosom; she flaunted her blue eyes, which were like two pools of water, just like her father's. She blushed and her long face which, when she smiled, appeared even longer and more drawn. She exhibited two rows of large teeth such as one only rarely sees among Jews, and she spoke with a startled, frightened voice:

"How do you do, sir?"

Volf shook her flat, dry, mannish hand; he didn't know what to say. The fact that the young woman was named Esther—a Jewish name—filled him with a sense of familiarity. She smelled of horses, the road, dust, and the female villager's shyness in the presence of men.

"Well," she shook off her embarrassment, "unharness the horse, Father, and take the packages from the wagon. I'm going to make some food and prepare beds for the gentlemen."

She worked hard turning over and stirring up the fresh straw that she was using to make a bed for the young outsider, devoting her feminine resources to the task. Every time that she caught the stranger glancing at her, she flushed bright red.

His coughing partner poked Volf in the side: "Do you like her?" he asked him quietly. "No great beauty, and she's not all that young, but she's worth committing a sin for. Don't be a fool, brother. Let's get out of here at daybreak. In the meantime, I'm going to get our goods in order."

He tickled Volf in the side, coughed a bit and winked.

Volf slunk away and sat himself down on the bed that had been freshly made for him. The fragrance of newly cut hay wafted in from outside. Crickets were chirping. Fireflies came in through the window with their little lights which were soon swiftly extinguished. Butterflies circled around the oil lamp and spread dust about. Volf listened to the familiar, nocturnal humming and buzzing; he breathed in the smell of milk, homemade baked goods, and beautifully preserved and pickled delicacies. It all filled him with calm and a sense of family. Overcome by the prospect of a sweet nap, he stretched out in bed which creaked under his girth.

At the crack of dawn with the first rays of the morning sun, he was out of bed and into the field. The farmer's daughter was already standing by the well, drawing water for the horses which were striving toward the bucket to get the first drink. Volf approached, helped her to hoist the water and bring it to the horses in a wooden pail whose edges had been gnawed away by the horses' teeth.

"This is the horse that you saved," she pointed to the young, strong horse. "Her name is Mary."

"My sister's name is also Esther," said Volf softly, not actually knowing why he related this particular fact.

The farmer came out of the house, glanced at the two people, and lit his pipe.

"You have a fine farm," Volf commended him in his meagre English.

"Do you like it?" asked the farmer incredulously, with a smile on his face that appeared whenever people praised his shabby farm.

"I'm also from a farm," said Volf, "far away."

He gestured off to the side where a sea would lie.

The farmer exhaled several dense rings of smoke and looked the stranger up and down. Then he abruptly removed the pipe from his mouth and hastily asked:

"And do you believe in God, young man?"

"Certainly!" replied Volf.

The farmer smiled and returned the pipe to his mouth.

"Perhaps you'd like to stay here, stranger?" he asked in a fatherly tone. "I'm old and Esther is a working girl, but still she's only a woman. The farm needs a man to work it, and I like you."

Volf looked first at the old man, then at his daughter, and shortly thereafter at the horse who nodded as if in agreement.

"All right, sir," he said with the gruff military r's.

Taken by extraordinary surprise, he had forgotten to ask about wages.

When his partner was going to leave, Volf gave him his bundle. The Litvak looked at him darkly.

"Look, you imbecile," he castigated Volf, "if you've got business with a *shikse*, fine, but you don't have to stay here. There are plenty of them on the road. Come on."

Volf blushed like a young man whom one groundlessly suspects of a transgression, and brought his partner's bundle to a wide road where he could catch a ride on a cart to the next city. He put the pack down there and, without a penny in his pocket—money which was properly owed him by his partner—returned to the farm.

"I've had my fill of dragging bundles around like a Tatar nomad," he said. "I'm going to stay in one place."

As he had long wanted to be on a farm, he went into the stable, chose the iron comb and brushes, crawled under a horse's belly, and cleaned off the dust from its hide, as he had done when he was in the army.

"Stop!" he said in Russian to a restless horse, using a word from his faraway home, forgetting that he ought to use the new language.

The farmer stood to the side, smiling at his daughter with delight at the young man's skillfully executed labor. Only now did he remember to ask the stranger his name.

"Volf," said the young man.

"Vulf, Vulf," the farmer repeated as if chewing on, and ripping apart, the strange name. "An odd name, don't you think, Esther?"

"Why?" His daughter failed to understand. "I like it."

**5**

# CHAPTER FIVE

Volf very quickly grew to feel at home on the farm and with the people there.

He arose at dawn and went to sleep at nightfall, at the same time as did the chickens in the yard. In overalls and with a wide-brimmed farmer's straw hat to protect himself from the powerful sun, he was, all day long, harnessed to his work, as were his horses. Although he still spoke his familiar, village patois to them, unlike the farmers who lived there, they—the horses, that is—quickly came to understand him, and they whinnied at him with joy when he arrived each morning at the stable to lead them to drink at the well. He stroked their heads which they extended to him, yearning for caresses; he scrutinized their eyes and their teeth, and taught them respect, as they were biting each other in the rush to be first to drink from the bucket of water.

"Halt!" he scolded them. "You're all going to drink, in turn. Don't fight each other!"

Afterwards he hitched the horses to the machine and set out for the fields.

"Giddy-up, children," he spurred them on, as he sat down on the small seat of the machine and cracked the whip, directed not at the horses but at the air, meant only to stir up their courage.

The work itself was rather easy. He didn't have to furrow the ground with a plow as he had been obliged to do back home, for the machine did everything here. A world of machines made for labor: machines to dig furrows and to harrow, to cut and to thresh, to do everything that needs to be done. One had only to hitch up the horses and lead them through the work. Volf was delighted with these machines, the likes of which he had never seen back home. He sang military songs jubilantly, snapping the whip to the beat.

The fields were expansive and vast, the horses healthy and well-fed. The sun radiated sheaves of light, rivers of melted silver flowing softly in the sky. Birds twittered. Field crickets persisted with their sweet buzzing. From time to time, a hare raised its ears in fright and beat a hasty retreat across the field. On several occasions, Volf forgot that he was in a foreign country thousands of miles from home. Everything seemed as it had been before. The same earth, birds, frightened hares, the eternally still, yet simultaneously rapid, life of the land.

"*Wiśta, hetta*" (Turn right, turn left), he said to horses in his own distinctive, Polish-equine tongue.

When the shadows emerged at midday, Volf unhitched the horses from their machines and went back home with them to eat.

"Where are you going?" he chastised the horses in Polish for competing with each other to get to the well, despite their being hot from work. They ought not rush to drink so soon after their exertion, he thought.

"Nice day, today, isn't it?" The farmer always asked the same question, as if his only concern was that the weather be beautiful.

"Very nice," answered Volf, wiping the beads of perspiration glistening on his face.

Esther, her smooth blond hair tied in a tight bun at the nape of her neck, had an apron tied around her slender waist. She had come out of the cowshed with a pail of fresh milk and poured it into porcelain cups for both men. She spread a colorful tablecloth over the rough-hewn table, put out butter, eggs, and assorted greens, and blushed every time that she met Volf's gaze.

"Nice day, today, isn't it?" she said, just as her father had, so as to say something . . . anything.

She had no other words.

"Very nice," he hummed in reply, also having nothing else to say.

The people there rarely spoke to one another. They were always hard at work. When they had time to rest, their mouths also rested. The old man sat with his pipe in his mouth, his light blue eyes peering out from his bony face. He smoked, spat, and said nothing. He could sit like this for hours at a time, silent, only rarely uttering a single word, one single word that would serve for all the others.

"Well!" he expelled the extraneous word from his mouth together with smoke from his pipe.

"Well!" countered and echoed his daughter, not averting her gaze from her sewing or knitting on which she usually was at work, whenever she was free from her chores in the courtyard.

Initially, Volf didn't understand these "wells"; he had no idea what they meant. Soon, though, he grasped their meaning and began to use the word, too. He said it on these occasions: when the weather was nice; when the rain came pouring down so that one could not so much as step outside; when work went smoothly for him; when something was stuck and no headway was being made. The second word which he frequently used rhymed with it: "hell." This one he used when he cut his finger in a machine; when a horse did not step into its harness easily; when a stone was left in the field and then banged around in a machine, as with every other hindrance that he confronted in his work.

Little by little he began to use other words which became familiar through the slow, muffled speech of the farmer and the protracted drawl of his daughter. Their repertoire of words was limited, a scant several hundred. Beyond that they were silent. Volf learned this speech as well as the quietude. He thus became used to living with his cigarettes and a branch whittled into a pipe which never left his lips. Just like the farmer, he tossed out words, askew, from one side of his mouth, along with the smoke from his pipe.

In his first few weeks, he had nothing to do on Sundays. The farmer and his daughter would hitch up the buggy and go to church in a town located a substantial few miles from the farm. After church, they would come home, and Esther would prepare a fine meal of meat, baked goods, and a rich pudding. She blushed as she proffered the plates heaped with especially large portions to Volf.

"How do you like it?" she asked unfailingly every time, looking at him with her mouth agape through which her long teeth jutted out.

After eating, the old man sat down in his chair and told his daughter to read from the Bible.

Despite the golden cross pictured on the cover of the black volume, Volf found that what she read made him feel at home. He heard a few things about the forefathers, about the Jews in Egypt whom Pharaoh tormented and for whom God commanded Moses to lead out of that land. It reminded him of his youth, when his teacher taught him the Pentateuch. What this sleekly coiffed gentile woman read of Jewish matters, about Abraham, Isaac, and Jacob, and about the exodus from Egypt, filled him with pride. He felt, somehow, exalted.

"Nice stories!" the old man commended to Volf the narratives from the Bible. "Do you understand them?"

"Yes, of course," said Volf smiling. "They're about my people . . ."

"That's right!" mumbled the old man and continued listening to more chronicles, as if for the first time, although he'd already heard them hundreds of times, every Sunday.

Although the day had elapsed with delicious and festive meals and reading, these long, quiet, yawning Sundays were nonetheless becoming tedious for Volf. He had nothing of his own to do. He hadn't stopped humming his military tunes and playing with the dog that nestled at his feet. He was anxiously awaiting the moment that the empty, lingering day would end, and people would, before long, get back into the workweek.

One Sunday, the farmer told Volf to get dressed in his new suit, a white shirt, and a tie. He handed Volf several dollars due him for his work and told him to hitch up the buggy and take it with his daughter to church.

When Volf drove up to the wide-open square where the church was located, he sat back down to wait until his bosses were finished with their prayers. Although he had, for some years now, from his military years on, eaten non-kosher foods, worked on the Jewish Sabbath, and had little to do with Judaism, he nonetheless believed that a Jew mustn't practice idolatry, and must not even enter such a gentile place. The farmer, however, unaware of Volf's taboos, grabbed his hand and led him to the door of the house of prayer.

"Come inside, boy!" he said to Volf.

Volf hesitated for a moment. His feet refused to budge. Esther looked at him pleadingly. Just at that moment, a young, red-cheeked man in civilian clothes and with gold eyeglasses approached the door to greet him.

"You're welcome, stranger. I'm the priest. Come in," he said with a smile on his face as he indicated the open door.

So, Volf then removed the straw hat from his head, as did all the men congregated, and went inside.

For a while he stood there undecided. He had never before been inside a Christian house of worship, although he'd caught a glimpse of a church once back home, as he was peering through an open door. He recalled the forbidding solemnity of the church, the numerous candles, backdrops, images of Jesus, the priests dressed all in white, the chanting by the gentile men and women, and more than anything else, the ceaseless ringing of bells. Something like fright commingled with fascination emerged from the desire to open the church doors: the fear of entering the imposing structure co-existed with the desire to enter it. He was reminded of the evils perpetrated against the Jews, of the troubles, calumnies, and their consequences: the baptized Jewish girls who had run away from their parents and their ancestral home.

There was nothing in this small church that Volf remembered from those back home. Only a few candles were burning and some lecterns were standing in a row. There were no icons there, no representations of little Jesus, no clerics in white clothing, and no bells. The people were quietly seated by the lecterns, listening to the sermon of the man in civilian clothing. The words were themselves familiar, concerned as they were with God and the children of Israel.

Volf opened his eyes wide. In this house of worship there was no hint of idolatry or gentile hatred of Jews of which he had been so fearful. It was entirely his own, recognizable and familiar. It actually reminded him of his small synagogue. Esther sat right next to him and pushed her prayer book toward him, just as his own sister used to ease a siddur in his direction when they both needed to read from the same passage. Volf felt a certain closeness to this house of worship, to the people around him, to the man in the civilian outfit who was preaching, to the girl at his side who in prayer was clinging softly to him. He recalled further that his sister back home was also named Esther. She sat right beside him, his boss's daughter. She was like a young Jewish woman, a relative of his own, despite her Slavic blondness and gentile height.

After prayers, Volf wanted to take the farmer and his daughter home, but the elderly man detained him.

"I'd like to walk home by foot," he said, "and you can stay in town. You're young folks. Have a good time! And, come home before nightfall, no later than that."

Volf turned the buggy around, seated Esther beside him, and, like all the other young couples, set out at a gallop through the streets.

Volf rode around the town with Esther the entire day. They peered into the storefront windows at the wares on sale. They observed the firemen who marched merrily along playing their trumpets. They ate a good meal at a restaurant where a longhaired musician was playing on an old piano.

"It's nice, isn't it?" Esther was wont to ask Volf throughout the performance.

"It sure is," replied Volf in English. Beyond that they had nothing to say to each other.

After eating they drove over to a wide plaza which was filled with carousels, a roller coaster, and all manner of entertainment. Magicians were plying their dark art. An Indian with long braids, like those of a woman, was swallowing fire and eating crushed glass. A half-naked Negro was playing with snakes and hammering nails into wood with only his hands. Cowboys with chaps over their pants were leaping onto horses and throwing lassos. Musicians, dressed like generals, were blissfully playing marching music.

Volf was revived with youthful energy. He bought several balls and aimed them right into the nose of a rubber Chinese figure, for which the surrounding audience applauded and the man in charge of the plaza, a man in a red Turkish cap, awarded him a box of sweets.

"Good shot!" Esther praised him and nibbled happily on the sweets that Volf passed to her.

Volf treated her to a shot at throwing the ball at the Chinese figure, but she missed. So, he took two wooden horses on the carousel, and around they went in a circle to the beat of the music. Over by the place where one could shoot at little ducks, Volf once again demonstrated his former military dexterity by hitting his mark. As a result all the ducks were knocked down for which he received as a prize a colorful plate with a group of hunters, ladies, and dogs painted in red. Esther was beaming with all the sparkling, large teeth in her open, jubilant mouth.

"It's wonderful!" she swooned in delight.

When they took seats in the roller coaster which raced up and down with head-spinning speed, Esther forgot her father and shyly screamed like all the other young ladies every time she went hurtling downhill.

"Whee!" she squealed and clung tightly to Volf's hand.

Volf held her firmly by the hand, her flat, boyish breast snuggling next to him, and when they shot down, headlong, into the darkness, he kissed her on the lips, embracing, just like all the other couples.

She was so unaccustomed to a man's kiss that she kissed him right back, more with her teeth than with her lips. At that point she was so bewildered that, when their seats fell under the light and every couple was pulling apart from one another, she was still glued to him, which provoked gales of laughter.

They returned home later than her father had requested. The old man was already sound asleep. The old-fashioned clock with the wooden cuckoo had already rung out the late hours.

"Oh, God!" whispered Esther to Volf in fear, as she scoped out the immediate area, the tip of her finger sweeping the entire room. "Father's going to be angry."

She made Volf's bed up on the couch in the dark; she was fearful that he might turn on a lamp, lest her father figure out what had happened.

"Good night," she said quietly, not moving from where she stood.

"Good night," said Volf, clasping her hand in a firm grip.

Silently, without uttering a word, obediently, as is demanded by one of life's commandments, they both sat down on the bed and fell into each other's arms. No feminine resistance was put up by this grown up, shy village girl to her man, the first such long-overdue encounter of her maidenhood. She was compliant and submissive to the strong, young man. To avoid word of their tryst getting out, they rose for work earlier than usual, well before the dawn emerged.

After several months, when Esther felt that her clothes were tight around the waist, and she could no longer withstand people's stares, she went to her father and broke down sobbing before him:

"Father, throw me out of your house!" she cried.

The old man took the pipe from his mouth, observed his supine daughter whose large teeth jutted out pitifully from her plaintive mouth, and said softly:

"Well, get that boy of yours to hitch up the buggy and get dressed. We're going to the sheriff for a marriage license."

Esther seized her father's hand and began kissing it.

"Daddy!" she cried out like a little girl whenever her father gave her a spanking she had earned.

The old man pulled his hands back and wiped them on his knees.

"Go now and blow your nose," he said firmly, "and wash your face. You look terrible when you cry."

Volf entered with his head bowed, eyes to the ground, prepared for the worst. But the old man remained calm, as always.

"Well," he offered at a leisurely pace, "Get dressed and shave. We are leaving now."

Volf lowered his head even further.

"To the church?" he asked in a trembling voice.

"To the sheriff!" replied the old man. "I'll show you the way."

Volf raised his head and went off happily to get ready.

The sheriff happened to be fixing a wheel on his wagon, when the bride and groom and her father arrived at his door. He put down his hammer and pliers, took off his overalls, washed his hands at the well, and donned his long Sunday coat to cover his weekday trousers. When they came to registering the groom's name, the sheriff found himself at something of an impasse.

"The family name is all right," he said, reading the Yiddish name Rubin as the English name Robin, "but the first name is funny, like the name of an animal."

Volf blushed.

"Don't worry about it, young fellow," said the officiant at the marriage ceremony, clapping him on the back. "I'll write your name down as Willy, as I would in a letter. You like the name?"

"Yes, sir," Volf agreed, as he always did when he was forced to exchange his old customs for the new American ones.

And, thereafter he remained: Willy Robin.

**6**

# CHAPTER SIX

Days, months, and years—one no different from the next, like drops of water—flowed by over the new soil into the life of farmer Robin.

His father-in-law was no longer alive and the farm with all the cows, chickens and other fowl, buildings, stables, barns, and workshop were bequeathed to Esther and her husband Volf, who for years now, from their wedding day forward, called himself Willy. She was not as neglectful of the farm as she had been before, when the old man and his daughter lived there all alone. Willy fixed the buildings, cleaned the old machinery, and bought some additional new machines. He also purchased a few young colts, as he had done back home, and would raise them to be big, strong horses. Cows and geese grazed in the meadows. From daybreak to evening, man and wife were harnessed to their work. Willy was in the fields with the horses in the stables, and in the workshop where he tinkered, cut wood, hammered nails, and greased, repaired, cleaned, and painted the machinery. Esther worked milking the cows, tending the chickens, and cleaning and cooking among the pots and pans in the kitchen.

They had no children.

She had miscarried the first child in the second trimester of her pregnancy, when she hoisted an over-brimmingly large bucket of water up from the well. She had not gotten pregnant again. Willy remained faithful to her, as he had vowed to do at their wedding.

She was thus engaged in work all day long, rising at dawn straight through until evening when they went to sleep.

Just as she had been an obedient daughter to her father, so was she now a docile wife to her husband, did everything that he asked, and was quiet, articulating not a word until he addressed her. She felt guilty for not having given birth to any children, although her husband never once blamed her in any way. To compound her sense of alienation, she did not feel close to her husband. She did love and respect him with a steadfast devotion as one finds in people who live in such a village or isolated settings. But she did begrudge him a wife's intimacy, as a woman does after giving birth to a child. She always blushed in his presence as in the days after they first met when he arrived at the farm. Rarely did she utter a word. She simply had nothing to say.

Willy was similarly reticent. Only when he was completely absorbed in his work would he whistle—and no longer the military songs he had now forgotten, but new ones, as do all young farmers. His work so consumed him that, right after eating dinner, he would collapse with exhaustion and sleep straight through the night without interruption.

The farm was situated off to the side, in a place where few people ever ventured. The surrounding neighbors knew that farmer Robin was a diligent workingman, a good proprietor, a quiet man with whom no one ever had any concerns, and that was all.

"Nice day today," was their greeting when they encountered him.

"Yes, pretty nice," Willy would answer.

When it rained, they told him that the weather was rather poor and he replied, "Yes, it is." When the heat was intense, they asked him if it was warm enough for him, and thereupon he would respond: "Thank you, it's plenty warm for me."

He wore a wide-brimmed farmer's hat, as did everyone in the area, and velvet trousers which were in good condition, neither shabby nor frayed. He puffed on his pipe and spoke with a farmer's pronunciation, yet with nothing to indicate that he was a foreigner. He didn't use many words, as was the case with most of the men of the land. He uttered only the words that he had need of, and no one any longer thought of him as foreign. People just forgot about his early, "green" years.

And, in the same way, did the folks back home also forget about Willy altogether, as if obliterated from memory. He wrote no letters home. In the early years, it weighed on his conscience that he was not writing or even thinking about writing. But, he would postpone doing so from one occasion to the next. Bit by bit, he forgot everything about the old country and now no longer even thought about it. Even in his dreams he no longer envisaged the past. And, he only very rarely dreamed. With little effort he would fall deeply asleep, like a stone, unconscious, when night came upon him.

As long as his father-in-law was alive, there was always an open road to the town that lay a considerable distance from the farm. The elderly man and Esther went there every Sunday for church, to which Willy had once accompanied them. After her father's death, Esther stopped attending church on Sunday. She understood that her husband did not go there willingly, so she remained at home, cooking and baking. Willy sat in his clean Sunday shirt and read the town newspaper which related bits of news, largely local pieces about the neighborhood, as well as the price of livestock and grain. When the elections came around, Willy would listen to what his neighbors were saying and vote the same way as did everyone around him. When he was once called to serve on a jury and judge someone who had broken the law of the land, he put on his Sunday suit, sat quietly in court, listened later to what the head juryman had to say about the matter, and voted to convict or exonerate as the majority voted.

He seldom went to town, only when he badly needed to do so. He would quickly purchase what he needed and return home. On rare occasions, he might stop for a glass of beer in a restaurant. Although there were a few Jewish merchants along the town's main street—a small number of businessmen who had earlier been peddlers—he avoided entering their stores. He never had any major dealings with them, not even when he trudged along the roads with his bundle. On rare occasions would he want to cross paths with them. He had nothing to say to them. In just the same way, he avoided meeting the peddlers who had lost their way hard by his farm.

There was nothing he needed. Esther, too, rarely had occasion to buy anything. She was a model of self-sufficiency: she sewed and knitted, mended items, and had none of the womanly appetite for colorful trifles and inexpensive jewelry that the peddlers carried around with them. The peddlers could quickly detect that there was no money coming in from this farm, and thus avoided the place altogether.

Willy thus forgot everything from before: his close relatives, and even the Jewish holidays had flown out of his head. He knew neither when they fell, nor which Jews living nearby were celebrating them. It was not that he was a non-believer. He knew full well that the world had not created itself, that all thunder and lightning, storms and winds, good and bad harvests, health and illnesses, birth and death, didn't just happen on their own, but were guided by God who resided somewhere in heaven. He rarely considered any of this. Such thoughts never entered his mind; even if they had, he would not have had time to entertain them. Like everyone, he often called out God's name, a mere word, one of many that he enunciated in the course of a day. He would say "God" in English, while not thinking of the creator, just as he would say the word "devil" and not actually be contemplating Satan. His life was moving along smoothly, like a calm river, engorged with his great effort and striving.

With the passage of time, he became more rooted to the earth, more a part of it. His hands had grown larger, his shoulders broader, his facial features coarser. The skin around his mouth had become furrowed with deep wrinkles as was the case with most men of his age and line of work. The pipe adhered to his lips as if it were an appendage. Esther similarly was becoming thinner and more desiccated with each passing day. Only her hands and feet had grown and become more masculine. Aside from the neighing of the horses, mooing of the cattle, clucking of the chickens, and chirping of the birds, one rarely heard a word spoken. Man and wife were silent, speaking only when it was utterly necessary. In the days of winter, when the opportunities for work were diminished, Willy would take the hunting rifle that his father-in-law had left behind, and off to the marshes he'd go to shoot wild ducks, or just wander around the woods to hunt a hare.

One fair, peaceful Sunday, when he was sitting before a juicy holiday meal and reading the newspaper, he happened upon a mention of his old home.

The town paper which always carried information about local incidents and the price of grain, had now frequently begun to offer news from distant lands that lay on the other side of the sea, where armed peoples were harming and slaughtering each other in wars. Together with the difficult names of French cities, mountains, and rivers, Willy also encountered more familiar names, the very names that he knew as well as the back of his hand. The names of the San and Wieprz Rivers, in which he had bathed and traveled by boat, were now featured in the newspaper. Enormous battles between the Russian and Austrian armies had erupted. Among the towns and villages that were mentioned, replete with mistakes, were also listed the places where he was born and where his parents and relatives had lived, some until this day. Willy took the pipe out of his mouth and remained sitting, helplessly.

"What's the matter, Willy?" asked Esther, startled when she observed her husband for the first time in such a bewildered state.

Willy handed her the paper and showed her the bad news. Esther choked on the difficult, strange names that became mutilated by her pronunciation, none of which did she recognize; she then, frustrated, just set the newspaper down.

"Poor people," she said casually, just as she once did when reading about a huge famine in China, an earthquake in Japan, or a flood in some secluded island.

She went back to her housework. Crestfallen as he was, Willy did not budge.

His home, his parents, brothers and sisters, relatives, acquaintances, all of those people whom he had forgotten all the many years he'd been on the farm, came back to him now, all at once, swimming up before his eyes. A longing—haunting and piercing—tugged at his heart. For the first time, his pipe tobacco had no taste; it was bitter as gall in his mouth. Esther brought him some coffee with a piece of cake which he so loved to eat every Sunday after dinner. She knew that her husband liked her to pour some milk into the coffee as well as some of the fatty, hardened milk skin, just as he used to drink in the old country. She never forgot to make the coffee for him in this his favorite manner. Willy touched neither the coffee nor the cake.

"Why aren't you drinking it? It'll get cold," Esther encouraged him. "Are you feeling ill?"

"No, I'm fine," Willy retorted coldly. He sensed an air of alienation from his wife, as she showed him no sympathy; nor did she understand that he had no taste for such things just then.

All of his grievances against his parents now flooded into his head and tormented him. Who has heard tell of them or knows their whereabouts? Perhaps they were no longer alive. Like a young hooligan, like a bastard son, he left them and never sent a word about what had become of him. One postcard he'd written, while still in Galicia, said that as soon as he arrived somewhere in the new world, he'd write. But he hadn't lived up even to this promise, not a single word. And, not a word had he informed them about himself. Only God in heaven knew how they worried about him and what catastrophic scenarios they envisaged! Especially his mother. She so loved him, always stood up for him when his father would chastise him for not wanting to study. They must have given him up for lost by now. Perhaps they'd even sat *shiva* for him and rent their garments!

He had tried to recall his mother's face, to see her as an elderly woman—for many years had sped by—but he couldn't conjure her up. He remembered her only at the moment when he left her and departed. It was harder for him to summon up from memory his father, sisters, brothers. Images of them dissolved as they passed before his eyes. He hadn't even taken with him any photographs of them, nothing of his own flesh and blood. Just the memory of a stony wasteland remained.

Willy personally felt great shame, as he did when he discovered he had done something ugly.

It was also true that they—his parents—hadn't behaved well either. He begged them repeatedly not to sell their farm, but to wait for him until he returned from the army and then, only then, would he set to work on it. They ignored him and sold the farm. They sold off the horses that he had raised with his own hands for a third of their value and, what is more, squandered the money on a shop in town that had not one customer discernible to the naked eye. It was not a good thing that his father had done all this, contemptuous of Willy's entreaties. So he could sit and idly gab with other Jews in the market, he'd turned an estate into a ruin and thus wasted and made a mess of everything. This was his reason for getting away in the first place. Yet he didn't have to cut himself off entirely from his parents, especially from his mother: she was guilty of nothing. She merely did whatever his father had demanded of her. He should have behaved like a proper son, letting them know of his whereabouts, writing a letter even just once, sending them a few dollars. Who knew if they had enough to live on? It was possible that they'd become ill due to various troubles, perhaps they were already gone from this world, and he, their son, did not even know of it, hadn't said *kaddish* for their poor souls. Possibly, because of their sins, they were suffering in hell. He'd left his Judaism behind, led the life of a gentile with no Sabbath, and no holidays. He did not even observe

Yom Kippur. And, he'd married a gentile woman. If they'd only known all this!

Willy felt a heavy weight on his straight and solid shoulders, so burdensome that, by contrast, the heaviest sacks seemed light as a feather to him. In his newspaper bitter news from his parents' town was recorded. Soldiers had entered it and departed. He remembered Russian soldiers, the Cossacks with their spears drawn who, even in good times, used to beat Jews when they encountered them on the road. They were murderers. It was now wartime, and who knew what acts they were perpetrating? They might well be burning and setting fire to his people there: his mother and father, if still alive, his sisters, brothers, and other relatives. In a time when he was sitting here safe and at peace in his own household, they had to run away from their homes which were ablaze, perhaps into the woods to hide themselves away. Perhaps, at this very moment, they are reaching out and begging for a piece of bread.

Esther shyly approached her husband and, with her rough masculine hand, stroked his shoulder in an attempt to bring him out of his dark mood. She didn't know any skillful way to manifest love for a man. Nor was she in possession of any tender words, any soft language. She understood that her husband was suffering because of his family in a distant land, but she was unable to sympathize with him in any meaningful way. Although she loved her husband and knew that he had come by himself from a faraway country somewhere beyond the great ocean, she sensed that it was altogether alien to interact with people from another continent who she had never in her life seen or heard. Nor did she know their faces.

"William," she said, "if you're going to drink the coffee, I'll warm it up for you."

She filled his pipe with tobacco and lit it, so that he could smoke it and forget his heartache. But Willy did not want the taste of sweet things in his mouth, nor did he want to smoke. Time and again, he picked up the newspaper and read about the battles in his old home.

From now on he no longer devoted Sundays to the section of the newspaper on the price of grain, but he went straight to the page of reports from the war.

One Sunday, in this spirit of true, real and honest reportage, he selected a pen and ink which were rarely used in his home. He poured several drops of water into a dry bit of solid ink so as to extract a little liquid tint with which he could write. He scraped some rust off the pen and sat down to write a letter home, the first such correspondence for so, so many years.

He tormented himself trying to recall the Yiddish alphabet that long ago had departed from his consciousness. His main troubles were with the *gimel* and the *zayen*, because he could not remember on which side each turned to a half moon—on the right side or the left.[1] In like fashion did the words seem strange to him, forgotten. After "My Beloved Parents," nothing further came to him. Erasing and staining the paper with ink—with more English words than Yiddish—he composed, with enormous difficulty, a short letter, one that caused him to perspire more than if he were harvesting, with strenuous sweeps of his scythe, an entire field. He went to his bed, under which he concealed his money in a straw sack, took out several $10 bills, and carefully inserted it into the letter, so that the postman wouldn't realize what was inside. He then hitched up the buggy and drove into town to buy an envelope and a stamp, neither of which had he ever kept in his house.

For the first time, he went in to the Jewish apothecary who had opened a pharmacy in the town. While buying envelopes and stamps, he asked the pharmacist about the war between Russia and Austria which was raging on in Poland and what people were saying about it. The pharmacist—a short, middle-aged man with limpid, thick eyeglasses, through which his eyes appeared to be twice as big and black—was laying out on the table colored pieces of soap in order, while he let fall a single Yiddish word in his Litvak dialect:

"*Tsores*"—"Troubles"—he said.

Willy dropped his letter in a mailbox with a trembling hand, as one would drop a treasure off a precipice; from then on he started waiting for the postman, but he didn't come. He did not bring a letter, nor did he return the letter that Willy had sent, on which the address of his farm was clearly written. Every time Willy had to be in town he paid a visit to the pharmacist and bought something, although he really needed nothing. He wanted to hear news from the other side of the sea. The pharmacist continued to lay out the pieces of sticky soap, as always, and he enunciated in his Litvak English-Yiddish:

"Big troubles in the old country. Yes, sir."

## NOTE

1. Translators' note: In their script form, these two characters appear roughly as mirror images, the gimel curving to the right and the zayen to the left.

**7**

# CHAPTER SEVEN

He did come—the postman, that is—with a reply to the Rubin farm, although very late, as many as four years having elapsed. On an envelope covered with numerous stamps, foreign and heavily colored—the sort never seen before in Russia—there was scribbled a poorly written address in chicken scratch-like, unintelligible letters.

The address was a feebly written mess. By contrast, the few sheets of paper inside were written with stylized, beautifully executed letters along cramped, dense, unspaced lines, every word adorned with dots. Willy easily recognized his father's handwriting, which was merely the vehicle for the same stilted and artful language that he used to write when his son was serving in the regiment. It filled him with joy. But, no matter how hard he tried to focus and distill something so as to read what was written in the letter, he couldn't do it, his eyes failed him. He'd long forgotten how to read his father's handwriting. His language was mixed with many of his father's customary words of Hebrew or Aramaic origin. He only just then noticed that there were several large and ungainly words attached at the very end. Willy recognized these as his mother's clumsy hand, and from this point he read more quickly.

"My beloved son, Velvl," she had written at the very end, at the edge of the paper, where his father relegated her to a few blank lines in his long, dense letter. Willy blushed. God, how long it had been since he'd heard his childhood name!

He read his mother's chicken scratches several times, but he still couldn't ascertain from her words what had happened to them. She had written only a few words—full of loving language but without content. The content must be in his father's precise lines, of which Willy could barely make out a single word. So, he hitched up the half-covered wagon, and although he had plenty of work to do on the farm, he left for the town to visit the pharmacist who he felt sure would be able to help him read the letter. For the first time ever, he snapped the whip to make the horses run more swiftly.

The pharmacist cleaned the thick lenses of his eyeglasses thoroughly and read the impenetrable pages of the letter for a long time.

"To my dear son, the longing of my soul, the apple of my eye, the honor of your name in its beauty, Zev Volf, your name should be lit up and shine," began the letter first in Hebrew and then soon switched over to Yiddish.

"Like a voice from heaven, your dear letter descended into our hands. Afterwards, inasmuch as we had given you up for lost and thought with great pain that you had estranged yourself, God forbid, from us forever, and we hadn't heard a word from you, a wonderful message arrived in these days of agony and sorrow. I was like our father Jacob, when they brought him news that his son Joseph was alive. So, I said: 'My son is still among the living!' I prayed to God in gratitude for keeping us alive to hear this wonderful news, and your mother—my predestined one, long may she live—said a prayer of thanks and cried from joy, and her happiness was without end. And, all of your brothers and sisters—may they enjoy long lives—and their children and friends as well rejoiced and thanked God. And, we prayed to God that He forgive the worry you caused us for so long, for due to your silence, we feared that, heaven forfend, we would go to our deaths with the grief of having lost you. . . . May God forgive you!"

After much florid prose, a mixture of Yiddish and Hebrew, with bits and pieces of scripture and aphorisms thrown in for good measure, whose tenor and flavor the pharmacist couldn't translate for Willy the farmer and his limited ability to comprehend, he proceeded to the news from home:

"'If all the rivers were ink, all the heavens parchment, and all the forests pens,'" wrote his father with a passage from a *Shavuot* hymn, the *akdamut*, "I would still be unable to describe in writing what we have had to bear during the years of war, perpetrated by the cutthroats and malevolent people who have laid waste to the tents of Jacob, and exterminated the best among us. Woe unto us when they razed our synagogue, and we were barely able to save the Torah scrolls. Woe unto our eyes which saw this: they hanged our rabbi—may his name be among the pure and holy—to the mockery and laughter of our enemies. These wicked men falsely accused him of having given signals to the armies of Kaiser Franz-Josef of Austria—all lies and slanders. They also shot many men of stature, among the finest in our community, as well as ordinary folk; women and children were not spared. Others were exiled far away in Russia, indeed so far that we do not know what has become of them. They set fire to the town, and Jewish property and belongings went up in smoke. We also lost everything right down to the laces on our shoes. Naked and in want are we now, and we are no longer young. . . ."

Willy wiped a tear from his eye with his calloused hand and tossed it on the ground, on the beautifully carpeted floor that sparkled with cleanliness. The pharmacist glanced at him from behind his thick glasses and skipped through several lines quickly, as one skips through the High Holiday prayer book when there are too many supplications to easily articulate.

"But blessed is God's name," he continued reading in a cheerful tone of voice, "that we have survived it all. For Jacob was not destroyed and his name was not effaced. We received news of you, our irreplaceable, beloved son. May God in heaven be praised for having protected you from every act of malice for if you had remained here, you would have had no choice but to go off and fight in the war. There is nothing bad that should not have a good outcome. And thus God made it so that you should be on the other side of the sea, so that you should be spared all the evil here—especially, as you are, thank God, a man who has succeeded in life, as you write, and you earn your sustenance honorably."

The pharmacist again skipped over a line or two, humming them under his breath, and then continued with the final portion of this long letter:

"'Son, my dear one,'" he read, "'there is no rest for us whatsoever. The curse for disobedience, all the reprimands and rebukes in the Torah—the *tokhekha*—have been fulfilled (Vayikra/Leviticus 26: 14–45 and Devarim/Deuteronomy 28: 15–68). 'All calamities have been earned. . . . One will drive out one thousand' (Leviticus 26:8). Despicable people who groveled and sought to earn a penny from us have arisen from the filth only to abase us. Our lives are wanton—they can do with us as they will—mockery and shame. Whoever can, has escaped to the other side of the sea. Therefore, we must turn to you and beseech you to have pity on our old age—save us from the hands of our enemies, for we no longer have the strength to bear all of this. The pain is too burdensome for our old bones. I have, of course, never assumed that I would need to seek help from a child, nor have I ever anticipated that I would need to leave my home in my old age and spend 120 years in a foreign land. However, it seems that God has willed it so, and there is no going against His authority. We would love to see you, my child, before we close our eyes for eternity, for we are old and broken. We have inquired with people who are experienced in these matters who have informed us that you can send for us. . . . We impatiently await the day when we shall see you and embrace you. Your father, who yearns for a reply.'"

The pharmacist was at a complete loss when it came to reading the ornate signature, as it was all but impossible to decipher. It was followed by greetings from various and sundry brothers and sisters, relatives and friends, all of which bore the same sentiment, and they squeezed in these insertions wherever there was a bit of empty space between the lines. The pharmacist, tired after reading this lengthy letter, wanted to skip over these salutations, as these strange names unclearly written and jammed in here and there were already too much for him, but Willy didn't want anything omitted and pleaded with him to read every word. In compensation, he bought a large number of pieces of aromatic soap which he had never in his life used. The pharmacist wrapped up the goods and praised the farmer for having such a father.

"Your father is quite a Torah scholar," he said in Yiddish. "His letter was full of references to biblical verses."

He looked the boorish village person over from head to foot and shook his head.

"America . . . go figure. The people you associate with. . . . I always thought that you came from a family of rough and tumble wagon drivers. I didn't even think you were Jewish."

Willy blushed like a little boy; ashamed, he went outside to the horses.

The next morning he caught the train and was on his way to New York to meet with some Jews there and to inquire what he would have to do to assist his parents. For the first time in all the years since he left with a bundle on his back, he would see New York once again—the streets, the people, the tall buildings, and the ruckus, including the clatter made by the elevated trains and the cars blowing their horns. He felt lost, as must every villager in a big city. As was his habit, he made his way to the East Side, where many Jews lived and where he had once wandered about aimlessly when he first arrived in this country. Just as in the past, laundry was hanging from every window and fire escape of the homes, most of which were red. Jews with pushcarts burdened with wares, were hawking their items for sale with voices, happy and sad. Children chased each other around on roller skates, throwing balls here and there and shrieking. Women were shouting and bargaining. Phonographs were playing cantorial pieces. Newspaper sellers were peddling their papers. Willy bought a Yiddish newspaper, which he had not seen in many years, and perused its pages. It was difficult for him to read, unaccustomed as he had become to it, but from the newspaper's large headlines the first word that caught his attention and that he recognized was "pogroms." He was sitting in a small restaurant which bore a large star of David painted on the window and the word "kosher" in it; he ordered something to eat. A stout woman brought him food reminiscent of a Sabbath meal: gefilte fish, white challah, chicken soup with noodles in which small reflective pools of fat were swimming around, a quarter chicken with the neck, and carrot stew. It was redolent of Jewishness and the old country.

Willy laid the newspaper down in front of him and, word by word, line by line, read aloud about all the sorrows transpiring on the other side of the ocean. What he didn't understand from the words, he understood from the pictures—pictures of violence and unhappiness. Among all the other towns mentioned in the newspaper, his father's town was recorded. American Jews had responded to the great appeals to do their duty, to support their poor brethren, and to rescue them from the repressive and murderous local forces.

Along the narrow streets with their cellars and shops, their religious bookstores and butchers, small study halls, and groceries, he noticed the amusing and colorful signs of various shipping agencies. In their windows, attractive posters were hanging, commending the tasty and kosher food that the ships served, as well as the synagogues in which to pray, under the supervision of great rabbis and overseers of ritual food and dietary laws. Nearby were hanging photographs of the supervisors, Jews with skullcaps and beards, men of stately appearance, one after the next. In another window people were preparing old clothing to be sent away to the needy. Banks were receiving money to send and to exchange currency. Lawyers and advisers had placed their photographs in the windows and were issuing an urgent appeal to those whom they might help with advice and official documents for their kin who wished to emigrate from overseas. People were pushing and shoving one another everywhere. The itinerant market was working at full steam. Speakers were addressing audiences from lecterns adorned with American placards, gesticulating wildly and calling for demonstrations against those who were responsible for pogroms aimed at their brethren.

Carried along with the crowd, Willy crawled around somewhere, disentangled himself from the rabble, and, in the midst of it all, sensed a great intimacy to something from which he had been separated since childhood. He found his own people here, like all the others, and this conveyed to him a closeness to the throng with all its hustle and bustle. He entered shipping companies and banks, listened to what people there had to say, and watched what others were doing so as to know how to comport himself in business affairs.

He was bewildered amid the great din. His faculties just didn't work as effortlessly as did the faculties of those around him. He couldn't simply go into an office and, just like that, settle on a course of action, as others were doing. He had to think about things long and hard and reflect on the matter a number of times.

For him it was not so much a question of the money involved, which he would have to deliver and for which he had toiled hard to earn. He was prepared to splurge to his last dime, whatever it would take to repay his parents for the pain that he had caused them. Also, he had no reason to continue holding onto his money. He had no children to pass it along to. Yet something bothered him. His parents wanted him to bring them to him, but he hadn't written them about his life, about the non-kosher house he sustained, and about his non-Jewish wife.

Esther certainly did not stand in his way when he explained that he wanted to bring his parents over from Europe. On the contrary, she was

delighted and looked forward to having her mother-in-law near her—
and her father-in-law, too. It would be very intimate in their home. He
showed her the picture he had of his father and mother, his father with
a skullcap on his head and a beard, and his mother with a wig worn by
most Orthodox Jewish women. But this elicited no extraordinary response from her, no flags went up. She noted nothing bizarre, as others
might have seen them.

"They look like fine people," she said with the simplicity of a village
woman for whom nothing could disturb her equilibrium.

Willy did not think otherwise. He knew his wife Esther well, and he
understood how compliant she was, how loyal and loving, and he was
sure that she would be a good daughter to his parents, too. But, he
wasn't so sure about the other side. What would they say when they
actually saw her with their own eyes?

He wanted to have a talk with someone about this matter, to consult
a fellow Jew and ask what he could do under similar circumstances, but
there was no one to offer advice. In all the offices before him, they only
sold things, dealt with customers quickly, and made a modest transac-
tion. Willy wandered around the area, bewildered, a lost soul among
this thicket of people. Then, out of the blue his gaze was arrested by
something. Next to one of the buildings, he saw a Hasidic rabbi, with a
full black beard, the traditional hat with a ginger-colored fur brim on
his head, and with a long, satin frock coat. Next to him was standing his
personal assistant and synagogue sexton, a slender little man with a half-
German and half-Galician style of hat. A woman in a wig hastily brought
a child over to the rabbi and placed his little head in a position so that
the rabbi would bless him. The rabbi gave his assistant his cane and laid
both hands on the child's head. Willy wasn't bold enough to approach,
but he paused for a moment. Although he was far removed from his
Judaism, he was not an unbeliever, and he knew that there was a great
God in heaven. In this man with holy garments, he recognized a mes-
senger from God who would show him the way.

The rabbi similarly recognized in this strange, tanned, and tall man,
a man of faith, so he extended to Willy a welcoming hand.

"Come upstairs with me. I live right here in this building," the rabbi
said.

The rabbi's home was appointed with inexpensive, amply uphol-
stered furniture, designed with starkly colorful leaves and flowers, and

garishly tinted lamps as one would find in vaudeville adorning the holy ark and the pulpit. Willy proffered the rabbi a dollar as payment for his advice and proceeded to recount in detail his entire crooked path— from his eating non-kosher food in the military in the past through to his settling on a farm owned by gentiles. He looked down reticently when it came to describing his gentile wife with whom he was living. He pronounced each of his words with trepidation, but the rabbi wasn't in the least impressed or surprised by his confession.

"So, big deal; what else do you have to report?" he urged Willy, impatient with his slow speech, itself a mixture of Yiddish and a farmer's English.

The rabbi was a sharp and proficient judge of people at a single glance, a cunning man who had for many years lived on the East Side; no confession in the world that came his way was the least bit remarkable. He knew America, as he did all the worries and joys of the present generation. Boys came to him, seeking advice about unrequited love, and girls conferred with him about impudent Italian pranksters with whom they had fallen in love. Women denounced their husbands who had affairs with other women, and married women confidentially recounted to him in detail the sins that they committed with other women's husbands and their heavy hearts which was the consequence of their actions. He had grown weary listening to the farmer's laborious explanation, the boring delivery of which was foreign to him.

"All right," he said in the language of the street, "what's past is past. But, what do you want to do now? Make it short. I'm very busy."

When Willy had at last expressed everything he meant to say, the rabbi sighed softly, his brow furrowed in a grid of deep creases, from his thick eyebrows till the edge of his skullcap.

"Do for your parents whatever they require of you," said the rabbi, switching to the less formal "you." "And, one piece of advice which concerns the gentile woman: she should convert, become a Jewess. You and she have no children together, right?"

Willy's large eyes glared directly at the rabbi. The rabbi had made of this whole matter small change, nothing at all.

"It's nothing for a gal," he said with a smile on his face. "It's more than enough for her just to learn a few mitzvahs."

Willy could scarcely believe what he was hearing, that it could be so easy.

"*Rebbe*," he said, "that's everything?"

The rabbi grabbed his beard and scoffed into it somewhat mockingly.

"In any event, there are Jews who are not Jews and gentiles who are not gentiles. Shabbat, the laws of keeping kosher, the marriage ceremony, family purity are not respected here at all. I mean, is there a difference? On the contrary, a gentile woman, when she comes to know these things, that is, when she has to light Shabbat candles and separate dairy and meat dishes, will observe all these things even more fastidiously. Just see to it that *you* are a good Jew!"

Willy was embarrassed by the rabbi's insinuation. The rabbi extended to him a weak handshake from inside his broad coat sleeve, a sign that he was busy, and then remembered to ask the woman's name.

"Esther," said Willy.

"A Jewish name," said the rabbi, overjoyed. "It'll be nothing for her compared to what our own Jewish daughters go through. It was predestined by heaven. . . . Go in good health and have much success!"

Willy was delighted as he made his way to a shipping company to speak about documents and passenger tickets.

# 8

# CHAPTER EIGHT

**E**sther, the farmer, in all her peasant earnestness, surrendered herself to her new female role which her mother-in-law, the old woman with the pitch black wig on her head, had labored to impress upon her.

Without a word in common between them, the wives both understood without having to say anything: on Friday at candle-lighting she would imitate her mother-in-law exactly by encircling with her hands the small flames, shielding her eyes with her palms.

"That's it!" my daughter, guided the old woman when her daughter-in-law did not remove her hands from her eyes.

"Gee," said Esther, self-conscious and embarrassed by her ignorance, her cheeks flushed bright red, as she smilingly and wordlessly beseeched her mother-in-law to forgive her lack of knowledge.

In just the same way, she learned to salt the meat before cooking it, as the older woman had demonstrated for her.

"Not so much salt, my dear," laughed the mother-in-law in her maternal manner. "One mustn't oversalt the meat."

She took a handful of salt, immersed the appropriate amount of meat in it, thus complying with the ritual of *kashrut*, and indicated to Esther how to imitate what she had done:

"I see, Mother," said Esther in English, and she took great pains to follow suit.

With the same faith and earnest devotion with which she had responded earlier to the dictates of Christianity, did she now apply to the new commandments that her husband had asked her to adopt because of his parents.

In the early days she did this for her husband's sake. She loved him—her husband—just as quietly and firmly as she had in those first days when he arrived at the farm. She was also truly grateful that he had not reprimanded her for not bringing children into the world, even though it was her fault. He didn't drink, didn't squander any money, worked constantly, and was completely devoted to her. She was, as a result, utterly compliant with his wishes, submissive and prepared to go through hell and high water for him. When he explained to her about his mother and father and asked her to carry out certain Jewish customs, she said not a word against it.

As far as she was concerned, no great sacrifice was being made on her part. If her husband wished it and it might bring some pleasure to his parents—who were going to be living with them—why would she not do it? In addition, all the new and rather strange things that she would have to do amounted to nothing too difficult.

Her wizened and hoary mother-in-law, although a bit odd in her wig which she wore over her closely cropped hair—Esther had never in her life seen such a thing—quickly became close to Esther. A former tenant farmer's daughter herself, she was quick to find life on a farm familiar. She milked cows, brought feed to the poultry, took eggs from the chickens, and performed all the other womanly tasks. Soon she removed the black wig and replaced it with a kerchief, as she had in the past when she was by herself in the village. This afforded her a different look, an intimate and domestic one. By and by, she earned Esther's love. Esther never had a woman near her—from childhood on she had been a motherless child. She was raised alone with her father on the farm. Nor had she ever had a child she could embrace and with whom she could demonstrate her motherly affection. Her father had been a reticent and hardened man, as is her husband. She had longed to have someone close to her, another woman. She was indeed overjoyed with her mother-in-law especially when she gave her a hug, her own head beside the soft bosom of the older woman who called out: "Esther, my daughter."

Willy translated his mother's words for her, so that she understood the phrase "my daughter." Esther felt a certain pleasure at hearing such tender words, the likes of which she had never heard from her own mother. "Mother," she said in English to the older woman and embraced her.

Although the old woman surmised that her daughter-in-law was not completely at home with Jewishness, that there remained something non-Jewish in her appearance and in her odd behavior, she made no issue of it at all. She'd been told in the old country that America in this regard was another world, that Jews are not Jews there, that everything there is topsy turvy and the best thing for a new immigrant is to observe and remain silent, because that is the way of the world. She did not know precisely if her daughter-in-law had once been a gentile or if she was the child of highly assimilated Jews who knew no Yiddish and were ignorant of Judaism. Nor was she like every gentile woman. First of all, her name was Esther like many a Jewish girl. Secondly, she demonstrated great love for her mother-in-law whom she called "Mama." She was also clearly redoubling her efforts to master the ritual components of Jewishness and soon she would, for the first time on Friday evening, light the Sabbath candles all by herself. And the old one had no complaints; she accepted everything, letting things evolve as they may. "What was past, was past," she reasoned with a woman's practicality. The main thing was that in the future the home should be run as a Jewish home.

The old woman simply unpacked her own pots and dishes, spoons and knives, that she had brought with her from the old country and which she had packed up with her linens, although everyone laughed at her and forbade her from carrying any bundles. She ignored them all and took everything with her: dairy and meat pots, and even the Passover dishes, packed in hay, as well as the Sabbath candlesticks and her women's prayer books in Yiddish, typically given to the bride by her groom, and *Tkhines* or supplications written in Yiddish. Now she saw that she had been right, that all these things would be of use to her. In the same manner, she removed the dishware and utensils from the packing, placing the meat and dairy dishes in separate places. She did all this herself, without saying a word, thoroughly heated up the oven so as to burn up every trace of non-kosher items, and she took over the kitchen, leaving nothing to her daughter-in-law for the time being.

"Go, go, my daughter," she said in her motherly tone and demeanor as she guided Esther from the kitchen, when the latter wanted, simply, to help. "I can take care of the cooking by myself. You've got enough other work to do. . . ."

Little by little, she taught Esther which pots were for meat and which for dairy: the knives with the notches in their handles were for dairy and the straight ones were for meat. Esther was confused, not knowing where to start or end, but the old woman spent a long time teaching her with gestures until she mastered it and strictly observed her mother-in-law's directions. In short order, she was able to properly salt the meat, protect herself from mixing dairy with meat and offer the benediction over the candles every Friday evening. In fact, she was incapable of saying something quietly, like her mother-in-law, while lighting candles; but moving her hands around the flames three times and then covering her eyes—all this she was as capable of doing as was the older woman. She even moved her lips quietly, although she knew nothing of what she was supposed to say. Her mother-in-law, sensing her struggles and best intentions, drew Esther's head to her breast in a maternal gesture.

On several occasions, Esther was deeply embarrassed for some act of foolishness that she'd committed. As she mistakenly understood that Jews need fish for the Sabbath, one time she brought non-kosher fish from the river and handed it to her mother-in-law to prepare. The mother-in-law put her hands over her eyes at the sight of this fish which had no scales and no fins and looked like worms.

"Oh, my dear daughter," said the older woman with a sour expression on her face. "This isn't kosher!"

Esther didn't understand, and the older woman had to show her with her hands what "*treyf*" (non-kosher) actually meant. Esther was overcome with mortification, like a young girl.

"Gee!" she said, ashamed, not comprehending the Jewish rules which would forbid such fine fish from being eaten.

On another occasion she brought home fresh, squirming crabs and dumped them out before her mother-in-law, so that she might prepare them for the midday meal on Sunday. The older woman began to scream in alarm, when she noted the wriggling, crawling critters. Esther again was embarrassed and threw the tasty creatures away. Both women could not stop laughing. And soon, Esther learned her way around Jewish practices; her mother-in-law very graciously allowed her entry into the kitchen. She became observant, applying excessive detail to her newly learned rules.

"Mother, may I . . ." she would always begin her questions about observance, fearful that she might introduce something *treyf* into the kitchen.

Little by little, she became completely immersed in these new customs and rules to which she was adhering solely to fulfill her obligation to her mother-in-law, though she was beginning to believe in them, like every observant person. She would execute a practice simply and seriously, with punctuality and rigor, not deviating by a hair right or left. As time passed, the two women began to understand one another. The older woman grasped a few English words, while her daughter-in-law learned several Yiddish words; they spoke in their free time, questioning each other and describing themselves to one another with details from their lives as women. Esther also became accustomed to the strange foods. They struck her as extremely odd initially—all the Jewish dishes, such as chicken broth with noodles, stuffed chicken necks, stuffed derma, greasy carrot stew, gefilte fish, and other fatty and sweet treats which her mother-in-law made. Esther quickly adapted to them all and even mastered cooking and baking a full range of delectable fare for a plethora of Jewish tastes.

Esther had a great deal of respect for her father-in-law, as she would for any man. She looked at him with a kind of imperceptible fear, as he sat in his lustrous alpaca suit coat down to his knee, with a velvet skullcap on his white hair. He spent his time looking through his gold-framed glasses at strange books, large and unintelligible. He appeared to her to be a clergyman. Not a single word could they utter to one another. Every time she brought him tea, of which he drank plentiful amounts, he smiled at her and nodded in assent, a sign that he wanted to say something, a kind word possibly, but he sadly could not—he was tongue-tied.

"*Danke, danke,*" he said in German, something he'd once heard from Austrian soldiers back home, during the war years when he was used to using a German word when he had to speak to someone who did not understand his language.

In an altogether familiar manner, he dipped sugar cubes in the tea so as to be able to bite into them with his old, weak teeth; with one sugar cube he could drink numerous glasses of tea.

Things were getting worse between father and son. Reb Hirsh couldn't get along with his own progeny, just as it had been back in their village, when Willy was a boy and wasn't following a straight and narrow Jewish path in life.

Now that he'd arrived in this new land, Reb Hirsh still perceived his son as utterly strange. Willy was all but unrecognizable, not solely because of Willy's clean-shaven face and short pants. Reb Hirsh knew from experience that, in this regard, Jews in America were not at all righteous. In the past it was the farmer's non-Jewish quality which rested comfortably on his son: the ruddiness of his face, the peasant boorishness that was simply not to be found among Jews, the pipe constantly in his mouth, and, more than anything else, the easy-going quality, quiet and sedate, and, most of all, his inviolable inner equilibrium. It occurred to the old man, as it had in the past, that he did not deserve such a son as Willy, as alien as he had become to his own Jewishness and to him, his own father.

Willy had wanted to bring his parents right from the ship all the way to his home on the farm. He had a great deal of work to do at home, for every minute was essential, as Esther, he knew, could not get everything done on her own. But his father just wouldn't listen. He had been personally handed numerous warm greetings by his countrymen to their compatriots in New York City. His pockets were stuffed with heartfelt letters from fathers to their children, from deserted wives to their husbands; he didn't want to leave until he'd delivered all of them, until he'd seen all of these people from his hometown. Meanwhile the Sabbath had surreptitiously crawled up on him and he couldn't go anywhere.

Willy was impatient; he couldn't just sit still while waiting around in New York. He detested the city and couldn't tolerate the noise and the racket which he thought he had already left behind. All these people with whom his father met were strange to him. They were older Jews, down-to-earth Torah scholars like his own father, who continually spoke of Torah and its verses of which Willy understood not a single word. And, to add insult to injury, they groaned and sighed audibly. They looked at Willy as if he were some sort of malicious marvel, and they always asked him the same question:

"What business are you in? Huh?"

"I am a farmer," Willy answered.

"You mean you run a boarding house," they would proceed to correct him.

"No, I have a farm," Willy held his ground.

The Jews regarded him and shrugged their shoulders.

"A farmer?" They didn't understand. "Really, literally? Like a gentile?"

As much as his father was completely at home among his compatriots, like a fish in water, so was Willy utterly restless among them. They struck him as bizarre—these fellows from their town in the old country—all of whom were asking after his health, line of work, and whether he could afford to support his family.

"How pitiable, how vulgar," his father continually said about everything that they asked him. "A Jew, penniless fellow, he should have—may there be no evil eye—a house full of children and grown daughters."

The Jews sighed, as if bits of their hearts were being ripped out of their chests.

Still lost and confused, Willy felt the Sabbath approaching when he and his father were invited into a warm, little synagogue where their compatriots prayed, and where they came to receive news and greetings from their town. His father was honored with the privilege of leading the congregation in prayer before the rabbi's lectern. In addition they offered Willy the honor of being called to recite the blessing before the reading of the Torah. Willy had no prayer shawl, and he remembered not a word from the prayer book. When the time for his being called to the Torah arrived—an honor given to him as a further tribute to his father—he remained standing there like an idiot, not knowing what prayer to recite. The Jews all around him rushed to his aid and prompted him with the proper words:

"Go ahead, 'Bless God Who is blessed . . .'"

He mumbled something under his breath, of which no one heard a word, and his ruddy farmer's face was ablaze with shame. His father glared at him furiously. He was just as much an utter outsider while sitting at the ritual meal after services which a countryman had arranged for his guests and the congregants. With his head lowered and his hands resting on, and affixed to, his knees, Willy was seated in a tiny, crowded room that was packed with furniture. He hardly touched the wine, cherry juice, and honey cake brought to him. The Jewish folk extended limp handshakes to his farmer's strong, overworked, and oversized palm and wished him all the best. Willy shook all the strange hands, not knowing what to say in reply. He was preoccupied with one thing only: his farm and its responsibilities which he had left on Esther's shoulders to bear alone.

When he was finally able to come home with his father and mother after the Sabbath, greeted by his dog who welcomed him back with exuberant barking, he was able to breathe more freely. He diligently unpacked the many bundles that his parents had brought with them. He made up beds for them with two mattresses stuffed with straw into every corner so that they would be soft for them to lie on. He aired out their bedding replete with many cushions and feather comforters, made their beds, and happily led his parents into their own separate room, which had been his father-in-law's bedroom.

"This is your chamber, Mother and Father," he said. "Make yourself at home. And don't worry. . . . Everything will be fine," he added, in a mixture of Yiddish and an immigrant's accented English.

He then remembered that his father did not understand the new language, and he took pains to use some familiar words.

"Don't worry, Father. Eat, drink, sleep, and that's all."

And, then, with the utmost energy he could summon, he tried to get back to his farm work, which he had neglected for several precious days, and threw himself into his labor with his fields, horses, and machinery.

His father, however, wasn't willing to sit complacently and eat, drink, and sleep, as his son had encouraged him to do, but launched into worries about everything—nor did he allow his son to calmly return to his work.

"Volf, where are the *mezuzes* on your doors?" he wanted to know about the absence of doorpost amulets. "I won't live in a house without them."

"*Mezuzes*?" he returned the question in embarrassment. He'd long forgotten that such things existed, that Jews used to have such items attached to their doorposts. In his broken vernacular, with more English words than Yiddish, he promised his father that at the first opportunity when in New York, he would pay a quick visit to the East Side where such things were sold and buy some *mezuzes*. He would be sure to buy some.

"Sure, shmure," the old man mocked his son's incomprehensible words. "In the meantime, I'll just sit here without a *mezuze*, like a gentile—let there be no such comparison."

For an entire week, he remained singularly silent. He hung about in the morning in an old prayer shawl and phylacteries, walked around registering which rooms of the house were without their *mezuzes* and rubbed his hands in distress.

"Master of the universe, dear Father," he uttered in the midst of saying his prayers and sighed as if a piece of his heart had been ripped out.

They ate dairy. Esther had wanted to slaughter a chicken and cook a proper meal for her parents-in-law, as one's proper guests deserve. But Willy warned her in advance that one mustn't do such a thing by oneself now, for one now needed a ritual slaughterer to do it—and such a man wasn't readily available in the village.

Thursday, in the middle of his most important work, Willy tore himself away and hitched up the buggy to bring home kosher meat from the neighboring town. He wanted to be able to make a proper, intimate Sabbath, and maybe make his father a bit happier and at peace in the process. But the old man had no desire to rest up in his new home. He insisted that his son take him along to the town.

"I'm interested in seeing what a kosher butcher shop looks like in this America of yours," he said eagerly.

In the well-appointed butcher shop, repainted white, in which there was not even a chip from a butcher block, stood a red-cheeked, clean-shaven man sporting a prominent moustache who, with his white apron and shiny knife, bore a resemblance to a genuine pig slaughterer. And, just as non-Jewish in appearance was his assistant, a portly woman with dyed, platinum blonde curls.

"What kind of meat can I get you, kosher or non-kosher?" asked the person in the apron.

"Kosher," said Willy.

The butcher set down the non-kosher knife and took the kosher one in hand. He brushed aside a piece of non-kosher meat and put in its place a piece of kosher meat, carving from it with the large knife.

Reb Hirsh grabbed the person with the apron by the hand just as he was slicing.

"Don't tell me that's the kosher meat?" he asked in a state of shock.

The man with the apron blew smoke from his cigar right into his face.

"I'm soon going to have no more of this," he said. "Only a few customers want kosher meat. The great majority buy non-kosher. There's no more business, so it's no longer worth the bother."

Reb Hirsh stood paralyzed for a moment. He had heard when he was back in his old home that Jewish life in America wasn't so wonderful, but such things his own eyes would not "believe." The old ardor of a man in charge, a good Jew, who lived to become involved in community affairs and in Jewish business, flared up within him:

"We should take it to a ritual slaughterer!" he began to scream. He was going to violate the Sabbath with a scene of desecration and such bizarre butchery.

The butcher laughed out loud:

"You're still new to this country, a greenhorn, old man," he said jokingly. "There are no ritual slaughterers here. I slaughter it, and you take it away."

"And, the rabbi? What about the rabbi?" asked Reb Hirsh impatiently.

"The rabbi sits with the priest and plays pinochle," laughed the butcher.

Reb Hirsh did not know exactly what this thing called "pinochle" was, but he did understand that it was certainly nothing good. The ruddy-cheeked butcher was lost in laughter at the old man's astonishment.

"This is not Europe here," he explained. "This is America. Here a rabbi eats ham and a ritual slaughterer sidles up to a *shikse*. . . . Yes, sir, everything is a bluff here, except for hard cash. And, that's all. . . ."

Willy had already packed up several pounds of kosher meat. His mother would ritually soak it in water, salt it, and prepare it as one should, but Reb Hirsh refused to touch it. His son beseeched him, telling him that he was in America now and would have to live like everyone else. The older man refused to listen.

"The Torah is the Torah everywhere—even in America," he mumbled. "I'm not going to sully my old age by eating non-kosher, impure food. The few years that I still have left—if you call this a life—I'll just have to do without meat."

Willy's father defied his own time-honored practices. All week long he roamed around in his Sabbath gabardine in the farmer's house with its large stone fireplaces reaching all the way up to the roof; he chanted the opening words of the buoyant *Lekha dodi*, with which one welcomes the Sabbath. He recited this prayer in the melody of the dirge one intones on Tisha b'Av, the ninth day of the Jewish month of Av, the commemorative holiday mourning the destruction of the Temple in Jerusalem. This praying all by oneself had no collective Jewish character. Off in a corner nearby, under a hunter's rifle inherited from the old farmer, stood his wife of many years, sighing into her women's Yiddish prayer book as she gazed sadly at her husband, the scholar. Her own father, an innkeeper, had once been so lucky as to get him to marry her.

"Observe and recall in a single utterance," groaned Reb Hirsh from the liturgy, as he looked upward to the rafters.

With the same melancholy melody, sung so softly that one could barely make out a word, she went through the blessing quickly, not over wine but over rolls, which were covered with the velvet challah overlay that they had brought with them from the old country. Esther had a bottle of apple wine placed on the table, her own homemade cider, but the old man had no desire to drink it. He didn't know what blessing was appropriate. So, he made the Sabbath benediction over the bread—a poor man's, ignominious benediction.

Willy couldn't listen to his father's laments. What did he want, the old man? That's what Willy failed to understand. He'd squandered both time and money for him, and insisted that his father do nothing, yet he continually groaned and whined; it was a disgrace for Esther that he wouldn't avail himself of the food she had placed before him. He was outside with the horses and the weekday noises were cursing while intruding on the Sabbath.

"Get out! Hell, get out!" echoed the noises intrusively through the window into his father's Sabbath prayers.

Suddenly, Reb Hirsh was overcome by a homesickness for the kind of Jews who had lived in the village long ago.

"Master of the universe," he pleaded, lifting his eyes to the rafters. "Deliver me from this village, and bring me back to be among Jews."

**9**

# CHAPTER NINE

**B**itter discord and arguments continued between father and son on the farm, just like in years gone by.

Although Willy had already reached middle age, with its attendant evidence of the first signs of gray hair at his temples, his father treated him like a young boy, as he had back in their village when he strayed from the proper path. He was forever instructing him in the performance of the commandments and in behaving with respectability. He would not allow him to eat with his head bare; he covered his son's head with whatever was at hand. And, he couldn't tolerate his son's whistling which Willy so loved.

"What is this with your whistling all the time, like an impudent gentile?" he scolded his son and plugged up his ears.

Willy simply failed to understand.

"Is it something I shouldn't do, Father?"

"Shouldn't? Should?" he asked, his face contorted. "It's just not appropriate behavior. How do you suppose it looks for a Jew to whistle?"

He would become furious every time that his son would sit down and play with his dog, stick his hands into his maw, causing the dog to bark with delight. The animal would jump up and kiss its owner's hands and face, and then run off friskily. Reb Hirsh couldn't stomach watching this.

"God help us," he said with disgust, turning his head to one side so as not to see the tenderness on full display between man and dog.

He was tacitly jealous of the dog. With his own father, Willy spent no free time at all. Reb Hirsh had always loved to talk, to chat about Torah, community affairs, and day-to-day matters. He was lonely here on the farm. He had nothing to talk about with his wife. With his daughter-in-law, he was like a deaf mute, unable to utter a single communicable word. And, he already knew by heart the handful of religious texts that he had brought with him. All day long, his son was away in the fields. He waited impatiently for evening, when his son would return from his work so that they could have a chat. But Willy was stingy with his words and he never stopped puffing on his pipe. To every torrent of his father's speech, he would drip a single word:

"Well," he would mumble in his easy-going manner.

The old man would become infuriated by his son's silence.

"Well here, well there," he'd say in anger and the stopped speaking.

Willy filled a fresh pipe with tobacco and went off to play with his dog. His father would be enraged by all this:

"When a father is a dog, then a dog is a father," wailed Reb Hirsh tearfully.

Embarrassed, Willy let go of his dog. The dog bounded toward the old man and placed its front legs on his knees, a hint that it wanted to play. With his elbows, Reb Hirsh shoved the dog away, like some ritually impure creature and cleaned his alpaca coat of dog hair that had stuck to it.

"*Pójdziesz, paszoł won*" (Get off of me, get away), he said in the gentile tongue of his former hometown, pushing the animal away, as if he were used to speaking to dogs.

Willy couldn't cope with his father. He had nothing to say to him. His father's stories about Jewishness, communal affairs, the joys and sorrows of small town Jews were alien to him. Incidentally, he was no longer used to hearing his father's language, understanding it even less, not knowing what he could say in return. On top of that, he had for many years on the farm mastered the art of being silent. In the best of all possible worlds, he had learned to make himself understood by the unspeaking creatures, the horses and the dogs. They understood him and he understood them.

Like every young person, he viewed older folks as dotards whose sole preoccupation was eating, resting, and sleeping. He saw the same concern among his farming neighbors, for when a father entered his later years and was unfit for labor, he would cease engaging in social interactions and would spend his time basking in the warmth of the sun and napping. Willy, though, knew full well that he had done everything for his father, and he wanted now to take a well-deserved break from him.

"Father," he said to him, "eat, drink, and say your prayers. . . . Esther will bring you 'tea.'"

"I don't need any 'tea,'" mimicked the old man mockingly of his son's Americanized speech, fire blazing from his eyes which shone with the energy and vigor of a younger man.

Just as in his town back home, he was drawn to other people, to community affairs, to being a big shot among men. He regarded himself a man of substance, a master in his own home. He was incapable of quietly observing the alien, un-Jewish undertakings of his son, who knew nothing of the Sabbath and holidays, nothing of any real meaning at all. Every time Willy did some sort of work on the Sabbath, Reb Hirsh smacked the table:

"I will not stand by and let the Sabbath be desecrated in my own house! I am the father here!"

His wife cut him down to size, undermining his conceit with her womanly common sense.

"Hirsh," she whispered in his ear. "This is not your home. We're staying with our child."

Reb Hirsh didn't want to hear this.

"Woman, I will not sell my soul for a mess of potage!" he said angrily.

And, when she wanted to enlighten him further, he stared at her indignantly.

"I have no idea how it is that I have begotten such a son, who does not even have the visage of a Jew," he screamed.

This whole business was becoming thoroughly tedious to Willy.

"Father," he said to him firmly, "there's none of that European business here about the Sabbath. This is America. There are no gentiles to help out on the Sabbath. Everyone is on his own here. The cows and the horses don't want to know from the Sabbath. . . ."

"A horse's hoof," said Reb Hirsh derisively, "that is, the horses are more valuable to him than his own father."

At this point Willy lost all patience. Nothing bothered him as much as when someone offended his horses. He started shouting words such as "hell" and "damn" so as to calm himself down. Reb Hirsh didn't know what his son's words meant, but he surmised that nothing good was intended toward him in these furious utterances, and he began weeping from the depths of his soul.

"Master of the universe," he cried out plaintively to God, "why did you not take me from my old home a long time before my last years, so that I should live to see such 'pride' from my own son?"

Willy was moved by his father's tears. Like every red-blooded man, he couldn't tolerate tears, least of all from a male. He placed his work-weary, calloused hands on his father's shoulders and gently stroked them.

"Listen, Father," he beseeched him, "it's the truth—I was a thick-headed, insensitive youngster. But, enough of that already. Be nice, old man," he added in English.

Several quiet days ensued in their home. Willy walked on eggshells; he was on his best behavior. He made sure not to whistle, remembered to wear his broad-brimmed hat when they ate, and chased his dog out of the house, so as not to enrage his father. Reb Hirsh, for his part, saw that his son was trying to accommodate him.

"Listen, it's okay, let the dog back in," he said with a smile on his face, when the dog clawed at the door and whimpered to be allowed back in.

Yet, before long, both men were back clinging to a tense yet cordial rapprochement. They were not able to resolve their differences so quickly. Father and son remained alien to one another and did not understand each other. As quiet a man as Willy was, taciturn and hard, with nothing on his mind of importance save his farm, animals and foul, so was his father restless, hot-headed, and entirely consumed by his own inner circle of cronies. Sitting there, he did not stop thinking about the bathhouse, his rabbi, the congregational trustees, and his own children and relatives whom he had left behind in a foreign land far, far away. Even strangers and distant family members he abandoned reluctantly. He continued ceaselessly to write letters home, on small, dense sheets of paper with ornamental, flamboyant, small letters, full of aphorisms, verses from sacred texts, Torah, all written in florid language. Willy, who scarcely ever held a pen in his hand, didn't understand what his father had to write about or why he was getting involved in the affairs of people somewhere on the other side of the world. He was somewhat nervous about asking, but he questioned his mother about it nonetheless.

"What is he writing about at such length, Mama?" he wished to know.

"It's because the entire community is on his mind," said the old woman none too happily. "He's always been that way."

Soon, Reb Hirsh began to hold forth authoritatively on Jewish subjects in the nearby town. The story about the butcher who sold non-kosher and kosher meat together brought him no peace of mind, and he could no longer remain idle on the farm. Every time that Willy went into town, his father would take to hanging around the buggy, like a child who wanted his father to take him along with him in the wagon. Willy had no particular desire to drive his father into town, out of consideration and respect for the horses. He'd never much liked burdening his horses unnecessarily. True, his father did not constitute a huge additional weight, but there was nothing positive to be gained from adding one more person to their burden. Willy also felt a little uncomfortable in full view of the neighbors. It was quite a bizarre sight in the eyes of the farmers: this bearded old man in the alpaca frockcoat and seemingly rabbinical hat which he had purchased for the trip to America. No one had ever seen such a person before. The older folks just looked on in wonderment, but the young boys and girls laughed out loud at the strange person in the outlandish garb. Others shouted after him words of mockery. This insulted Willy deeply. He enjoyed spending time in the town, the old man did, looking up Jews who were drawn to him; afterward he was not anxious to return home at the assigned hour.

"In just a little while, Volf," he would beg off, as a delaying tactic, when his son called him back to the buggy. "It's been an entire week since I've seen a Jew with my own eyes."

He loved to engage in disputes with the pharmacist who had read his learned and overwrought letter for Willy and to whom Willy had once introduced him. The druggist, with his thick lenses, was a *Maskil*, an "enlightened" Jew who had once studied in a *yeshiva* in Lithuania. Although he had long been living in the United States, he still truly enjoyed trotting out his past learning and exchanging views on passages from the Torah, which he retained in full in his capacious memory. While this pharmacist was indeed a non-believer, having disavowed both God and the Messiah, Reb Hirsh much appreciated, and genuinely thirsted for, the man's sharp intellect and learning. He sought him out to try to have him change his mind for the better, through all manner of parables and proofs drawn from religious texts. The druggist would not allow such an eventuality to transpire. With the pieces of fragrant soaps lying on the counter, he would blurt out before the older man an entire world of Torah, which he used to sustain his non-belief. Reb Hirsh said, in a fuming rage:

"That's exactly it, Mr. Litvak miscreant! What do you know? You simply hold on to your views which come from nowhere: you know, but you don't believe! You're just a heretic. May your abominable name be effaced for all time."

Berating each other, rebuking one another for their respective unthinkable and untenable belief systems, the two men became very close, cleaving to one another. Yearning for a word of Torah, they both longed equally for some manner of Jewishness in this ignorant, God-forsaken American town. Through this pharmacist, Reb Hirsh discovered other Jews in the town, several fathers with their increasingly assimilated, upstart children—men who used to work as peddlers and now were businessmen. Just like Reb Hirsh, they were estranged from their children in their own homes and were afraid of touching any food because everything was non-kosher to the bone. Reb Hirsh came back to life when he saw comparable cases around him. With his breadth of Torah learning, he was, in their eyes, the cream of the crop: a true scholar and sage.

One day he inquired after the local rabbi and successfully tracked him down at his home. He was received by a tall, young, clean-shaven gentile man with blond, slickly combed hair. While Reb Hirsh had already heard from the butcher that the rabbi sat and played pinochle with the priest, Hirsh nonetheless stood there saying nothing, when the young, gentile man came out to greet him.

"I need to see the rabbi," he stammered in a Germanized Yiddish, so as to be better understood. "I am the rabbi," replied the clean-shaven, blond, young man in an Americanized Yiddish. "Come in."

Like every American-born person wishing to speak Yiddish, he immediately used the informal "you," not the more deferential and respectful "you" accorded one's elders.

Reb Hirsh inwardly sensed a warm and familiar man of the community, who, when it comes to his own Jewishness, respects no border nor balks at any obstacle, so he set out with sharp words, as he had done in the town, with an argument for the rabbi.

"Rabbi," he said, using the Germanized term so as not to employ the appropriate and honorific term, *rov*, for this man with his shaved gentile face. "I have come to pick a quarrel with you."

And, then, not waiting for a single word of response, he began to speak like a firebrand about the butcher shop in which kosher and non-kosher meats lay side by side, woe to the eyes that would see such a thing.

The blond rabbi listened passively to the old man's deluge of vitriol and did not interrupt him with so much as a single word. When the old man finally finished what he had come to say and calmed down, he invited Reb Hirsh to take a seat and with a smile appeased him:

"'Wise men speak with great ease,'" he said in Hebrew with Sephardic enunciation—"without 'excitement.'" "Nothing is accomplished with screaming. Let's speak about this quietly. I'll be glad to listen to you," he added, the last sentence in English.

Reb Hirsh was dumbfounded by the blond man's Hebrew aphorism, as if he had heard a word of Yiddish from a gentile, and he began to speak of Torah and Judaism, exhibiting his full range of Torah learning so as to show this man, this American, that he was not some worthless and ignorant boor. The rabbi complimented him and once again invited him in. Willy had had any number of times to crack his whip before the rabbi's window until his father came out to the buggy.

"I told him the story, this 'rabbi' of yours, Volf," bragged Reb Hirsh. "I told him off, about how things should be, and I wasn't at all bashful about it."

He looked with an imperious glare through his golden-framed glasses to see what impression his speech would have on his son.

Willy, though, wasn't the least bit impressed by his father's boastfulness. Waving the whip in his hand—not, heaven forbid, on the horses' hides, but only in the air to urge them on—he emitted a few, indecipherable words together with the smoke from his pipe:

"Mind your own business, old man," he said in English, adding a lesson in the American way of life in Yiddish: "This isn't Europe. Everyone is only for himself here, Father."

**10**

## CHAPTER TEN

**S**trange people—the likes of whom had never been seen in the neighborhood—began to appear along the desolate, poorly paved road which led to Willy's out-of-the-way farm. Before the question was even asked, the farmers nearby showed these strangers how they were best advised to go.

First to arrive was the druggist with the thick-lensed glasses, through which his eyes seemed to grow to twice their normal size. Every Sunday he'd leave his store in the hands of an assistant, and in his old Ford—clearly on its last legs, though showing signs of its vibrant, once-green color—he would set out to visit old Reb Hirsh. He would have a discussion with him about Torah and worldly matters, whose mutual contemplation and discussion with his peers he would miss while spending a full week among his bottles and soaps. A near-sighted, heavy-set man with short arms and legs, he bounced along in his old vehicle, often over-zealously giving signals on all sides so that no one would brush against his old jalopy lest it explode. Every time he'd forget the tortuous route to this distant farm, and every time the farmers would show him the route he needed to take.

Reb Hirsh went out to greet him with open arms.

"He has arrived, the Litvak heretic," he said joyfully. "It is alleged that he will actually take a seat this time."

"Do you suspect that I will be desecrating the Christian Sabbath?" said the pharmacist lightheartedly, as he frightened all the dogs in the yard with his broad gestures.

Willy took a dim view of the druggist's visits to his farm.

"How do you do?" he murmured under his breath at the Litvak's playful greetings which were repeated time and again and Willy took off for his stables.

For his part, the pharmacist was being completely genuine. He neither saw anything sharply through his thick glasses, nor did he make much of the fact that a young farmer was muttering with dissatisfaction there. He launched right into his debates over Torah with Reb Hirsh and picked up his interrupted conversation that remained precisely where he had left it the previous week.

"If I remember correctly, weren't we in the midst of a discussion about Maimonides last week?" he said, pleased with himself at his proficient memory. "Is that right, Reb Hirsh?"

"Yes, that's right, you scoundrel," said Reb Hirsh, nodding in assent. "You have a mind like a steel trap."

Meandering around the meadows and fields, they quarreled loudly about passages from the Torah or the Talmud, each reprimanding the other bluntly. The two women placed tasty dishes on the table for their guest. The druggist ate like it was his last meal, beside himself with lavish praise for these women who had cooked such delectable home-made dishes. After eating, he offered the standard quip to Willy:

"As long as we are in sufficient numbers," he said in jest, "would you lead us in the grace after the meal? Come on, boy!" he added in English.

As he was leaving, he repeated the same story as he did every week. The druggist grabbed his wallet, wanting to pay something for the food, and Reb Hirsh swore up and down that he would simply not allow such a thing to happen.

"Am I to suppose that you're running some sort of 'boarding house' here?" the pharmacist contended. "Why should I not pay something?"

"Speak no more. You're humiliating me," replied Reb Hirsh. "You are my guest, and I am delighted to see you when you come here."

Lest he depart empty-handed, the pharmacist always bought some fresh eggs, a bottle of honey straight from the beehive and some vegetables to bring home.

"Good-bye, ladies and gentlemen," he called out in English from his car, which was disgorging numerous blasts of smoke. All the while he was waving salutations.

Shortly thereafter others from the town followed suit, dropping in for a quick visit.

Among his acquaintances in the town, Reb Hirsh met a Jew the same age as himself whose son, the owner of the largest clothing store, had not long before brought him over from the other side of the ocean. The old Jew felt utterly strange in the lavish, gaudy house of his nouveau-riche son, spinning around like a shadow amid his grandchildren who collectively knew not a word of Yiddish. He wept alone all day long and begged his son to purchase passage for him to return home. However, his son was in no rush to send his father back to Europe. He wanted to give him a "good time," and one Sunday when he was free from business affairs, he took his father in his new automobile and headed out for the farm. It would be an opportunity for him to speak freely with Reb Hirsh.

The son did this initially as an exacting obligation to his father, the ancient bore, but being on the farm was like a burst of fresh air owing to the peace and quiet of the rural area. The fresh air made him hungry immediately. The food served by the women at the table was both tasty and familiar. Upon leaving, he left too much money, a full ten dollars, for the food. Esther didn't actually want to take it, but the businessman thrust it directly into her hand.

"I'll come again," he cried out in English from the automobile. "It's a nice place you have here."

After him, other businessmen started taking their old fathers and mothers to the farm on Sunday, taking their old clothes out for an airing whenever they had a free day.

In new, shiny cars, as if just then having received a fresh coat of paint, with assurance and considerable din, they drove into the isolated farm and settled themselves in, as if in their own home. Willy frowned on all these strange folks. In great numbers, they were everywhere, creeping around the stables, walking around in the meadows, marveling at everything, asking questions. Soon they'd start singing songs, riding horses and sailing boats along the brook. Willy was not about to offer them any of his horses. These people could not even understand him, after all.

"All right," they'd say, "we'll pay you a dollar. Money is of no consequence."

Just as Willy walked around disgruntled, so did Reb Hirsh beam with joy; he felt right at home, like a fish in water. He spoke about Jewishness and secular things, talked endlessly about Torah and learning to these people who are all decked out in fancy clothing in an effort to show them that he, a recent immigrant, had such a depth of knowledge, of which they, the Americans, knew nothing, firmly entrenched in this ignorance. They truly admired him, these plump businessmen; in their ignorant humility they listened to his erudite teachings. They understood not a word of it, and pointed out to their children, their "illustrious" descendants, in English:

"You see how smart the old people are."

Reb Hirsh's wife had demonstrated her knowledge as a cook, having made chopped liver, herring with onions, chicken soup with fat, and stuffed chicken necks, all of which these wealthy people thoroughly enjoyed.

"Delicious," they all praised the cooking, as they savored every last bite of the old Jewish fare.

This was a quiet respite after the bloody "steaks" and "chops" with greens that their black maids prepared for them and with which they were thoroughly fed up.

As they were leaving, they'd buy some eggs and fruits, as well as bouquets of flowers, and pay more than Esther asked. They'd shake Reb Hirsh's hand for a long time, having harangued him about Judaism, about *kaddish* (the prayer for the dead said by relatives), and about prayers for the souls of the departed, as they would before a rabbi. What is more, they would promise to keep a kosher kitchen and cherish their Jewishness. On many occasions, Reb Hirsh would even assemble a quorum of ten adult males and finish reciting the afternoon devotions at a prayer lectern, just like in the old country. Esther would stand there with an earnest piety, with both of her rough hands folded over her modest chest, listening to the strange words of the prayers which she understood not at all.

Willy was grumbling about all this, but Esther quieted him. She passed him the small bundles of money that they had earned in a single day—more than for a whole week of hard work on the farm—and she would not allow him to say a single bad word about the guests.

"They are fine people," she said.

She had become so attached to this new life that she actually looked forward to Sunday, when the people from the town would arrive. She looked upon her father-in-law with great admiration, as she would a clergyman. He had truly grown in her estimation, when the town rabbi himself came by to visit. He spoke sweetly with her, Esther, words of the Bible, praised her for her piety and called her "daughter." Esther blushed with both shame and tenderness. She held her father-in-law in such high esteem that she always stood by him when Willy became angry with him for filling his son's head so full of Jewish ideas and customs. A number of times, when in the middle of the week the old man was overcome by a fierce desire to see Jews and Willy was not eager to drive him into town, Esther would hitch up the buggy and go with him. Reb Hirsh smiled at her in a paternal way from behind his golden-framed glasses and shook his head affirmatively, a sign indicating that he would like to speak with her, though he sorely lacked the words in English.

# CHAPTER ELEVEN

**R**eb Hirsh's letters to his town back home were not in vain. He wanted to have Jews around him, and this he indeed accomplished.

Before the first High Holy Days as Reb Hirsh had accurately calculated, his older son—his firstborn—arrived with a large number of children, bags, and assorted things. Amid all the other baskets and boxes which he brought with him, he was guarding one special box very closely: within it lay a Torah scroll wrapped in a prayer shawl. This was Reb Hirsh's scroll which was turned around carved wooden rollers, with a silver pointer for reading from the Torah scroll hanging from its decorative velvet mantle.

"Gently, Volf, slowly," warned his own brother, this bearded Jew, whom Willy would never have recognized, when he carried down the box in question. "There is a Torah scroll inside. Don't drop it, God forbid!"

A boisterous and voluble man, just like his father, this new arrival was buzzing around his numerous children and objects, running from one to the next, counting his packages and discharging words, rapidly and intertwined, flowing from one thing to the next.

"This one? This is Volf?" he could not stop marveling. "He seems to have turned into a gentile in this America."

While unpacking his things, he reeled off copious greetings from all manner of aunts, uncles, and cousins whom Willy had long forgotten. He recounted how they eked out their meagre subsistence, their troubles with their children, and ended with a sigh:

"They all want to come here. They're already preparing for the trip."

Reb Hirsh placed his Torah scroll in his small prayer room and instructed his son to remove the hunter's rifle hanging on the wall.

"Such a thing egregiously dishonors the Torah," he mumbled, "and what do you need it for, Volf? It's not something for a Jew to own."

Because of the new guest the pharmacist came out to the farm at Rosh Hashanah. In addition, Reb Hirsh's acquaintances from the town came so as not to take part in the prayers in the town's synagogue with its clean-shaven cantor. Reb Hirsh put together a decent quorum, led all the prayers by himself from the lectern, as well as read from the Torah. The Jews were beside themselves with delight at the beauty of his prayers and Torah reading. Even the druggist, the heretic, was part of the *minyan*. In the next room over through an open door, covered with a bed sheet, giving it the respectable appearance of a women's synagogue, stood the women praying with the holiday prayer books. In a festive dress, with a white shawl covering her head, Esther listened attentively to the strange High Holy Days melodies; she piously whispered and mimicked the chants, unable to identify a single word.

With his house now having become crowded with strangers and newcomers, Willy began to build and mount an additional floor to his home. Initially he tinkered, hammered, and assembled pieces by himself, but because he had too much of his own work to do, he hired several craftsmen. They rebuilt and enlarged the house beyond recognition. It was now distinguished from all the neighboring homes. Later, they painted it red, and the shutters green. When all the work was completed, they painted a large white signboard over the red exterior wall with the name of the owner: "Willy's Summer Place," in lovely, ornate lettering. Under it they placed a Star of David and right in the middle they fit the word "kosher."

Now, cars arrived even more frequently. Reb Hirsh wrote letters frequently to family members across the sea and, with the arrogance of a landowner, walked around the yard in circles with his hands inserted firmly into the pockets of his alpaca coat.

"With God's help, Volf, we should have several *minyonim* of Jews," he said. "We will need to explain everything in intimate detail to our rabbi in the town back home, let there be no doubt about it."

Willy threw a sullen look at the proliferation of new automobiles which heightened his instinct to protect the chickens, cattle, and horses.

Inhaling the strong gasoline fumes fouling the air, he left without saying a word to look in on his horses in the stables.

He thought hard about taking off from there, as he had years before from the town back in Europe, when he unexpectedly left one night from home and stole across the border.

The horses stretched out their necks to Volf, the better to be caressed by him, as they neighed in his direction, longingly.

# ABOUT THE TRANSLATORS

**Joshua A. Fogel** has a BA from the University of Chicago and an MA and PhD from Columbia University. He is Canada Research Chair and professor of History, York University, Toronto. His research interests concern the cultural dimension of Sino-Japanese relations, Yiddish biography, and translation as a practice. He is founding and continuing editor of the online journal, *Sino-Japanese Studies*. He has held grants from the Fulbright-Hays Commission, the Japan Foundation, the Japanese Ministry of Education, the Social Science and Humanities Council of Canada, and other agencies. He is the author, editor, or translator of sixty-five books. His major works include: *A Friend in Deed: Lu Xun, Uchiyama Kanzō, and the Intellectual World of Shanghai on the Eve of War* (2019); *Japanese for Sinologists: A Reading Primer with Glossaries and Translations* (2017); *Maiden Voyage: The* Senzaimaru *and the Creation of Modern Sino-Japanese Relations* (2014); *Japanese Historiography and the Gold Seal of 57 C.E.: Relic, Text, Object, Fake* (2013); *Articulating the Sinosphere: Sino-Japanese Relations in Space and Time* (2009); *The Literature of Travel in the Japanese Rediscovery of China, 1862-1945* (1996); *The Cultural Dimension of Sino-Japanese Relations: Essays on the Nineteenth and Twentieth Centuries* (1994); *Nakae Ushikichi in China: The Mourning of Spirit* (1989); *Ai Ssu-ch'i's Contribution to the Development of Chinese Marxism* (1987); and *Politics and Sinology: The Case of Naitō Konan (1866-1934)* (1984).

**Linda/Leye Lipsky** holds a BA and MA from McGill University and a PhD in literature and philosophy from L'Université de Montréal. She teaches literature, part time, in the Department of Humanities at York University, Toronto. Among the courses she has taught: Yiddish Modernist Poetry in Translation; Modern Yiddish Fiction in Translation; Yiddish Language; Modernism Across the Arts; Literary Responses to the Holocaust; and Seventeenth to Nineteenth Century American Literature. She has a specific interest in all manner of Yiddish poetry and poetics, the interrelations of literature and philosophy, and the crosscurrents of poetry and the visual arts. She has written critical appreciations of Avrom Liessin in the *Encyclopedia of the Bible and Its Reception* (2018) and of Beyle Schaechter Gottesman: "Dem oyle regls tokhter: The Poetic Pilgrimage of Beyle Schaechter-Gottesman," *Czernowitz at 100: The First Yiddish Language Conference in Historical Perspective: Proceedings of the Conference*, Joshua A. Fogel and Kalman Weiser, eds. (2010); *Jewish Women: A Comprehensive Historical Encyclopedia*, Moshe Shalvi, ed. (2006); "Nusakh Beyle," *Afn Shvel* (2006). She has written original works of Yiddish poetry published in *Afn Shvel*, special literary volume (2013) and in *Vidervuks: a naye dor yidishe shrayber* (1989). Among her conference presentations: Delmore Schwartz and his interest in Husserlian phenomenology for NEMLA. She has organized a panel on Canadian perspectives on Yiddish translation for AJS, and is the recipient of an award from the Social Sciences and Humanities Research Council of Canada and a research and teaching development grants from York. She is a contributor to a volume of translations of Lily Berger's Yiddish biographical essays, short stories and cultural reflections (in progress).

www.ingramcontent.com/pod-product-compliance
Lightning Source LLC
Chambersburg PA
CBHW060557100726
47907CB00005B/1407